Keeping Faith
TJ Vertigo

Keeping Faith

TJ Vertigo

Affinity
eBook Press
NZ
2016

Keeping Faith

© 2016 by TJ Vertigo

Affinity E-Book Press NZ LTD
Canterbury, New Zealand

1st Edition

ISBN: 978-0-908351-74-9

Editor: Nat Burns
Proof Editor: Alexis Smith
Cover Design: Irish Dragon Designs

Acknowledgments

This book wouldn't be possible without Mel and Julie from Affinity, thank you ladies. A special thank you goes to Nancy K...You rock!

Dedication

This book is dedicated is to all the Reece and Faith fans out there; and to my loyal fans, who had my back from the start. I can't thank you enough.

Table of Contents

Also by TJ Vertigo

Caution: Under Construction

Private Dancer

Hidden Desires

Reece's Faith

Reece's Star

Chapter One

Faith Ashford stood in front of the full-length mirror, staring at her reflection.

This skirt is too short, she thought as she yanked it down in the back.

She shook her head in sudden disagreement with her blouse, threw open the closet door and bit her bottom lip.

A few months ago, the actress had been offered her second role in a movie, an independent feature that looked promising. It was playing the role of a lesbian, a rather complex part, in which the heroine actually comes out on top. The openly gay actress absolutely loved the part and being told that it had been written specifically for her, thrilled her.

Yet word about the part had somehow gotten out and the bigwigs in charge had been flooded with calls. Since playing a lesbian in a movie was considered ultra-chic, the big stars all seemed to want the juicy role. Agents pushed their top name clients, and before anyone could control it, the role had taken on a persistent life of its own. To appease the masses, an audition was set up, with full reassurance to Faith that, no matter who did a reading, she would still get the part.

Still... Faith was a nervous wreck.

What if Demi Moore or Jennifer Lopez reads for it? Surely they'll get it instead of me, she silently agonized.

Names like those could bring an independent film the kind of notoriety that could benefit them, big time. Faith was beyond worried. She had nothing to prepare herself, no script to study, nothing. She was going to this audition blindly, on the word of her agent, Brad Rogers, and a man named Bill that she'd met at a cocktail party.

†

Reece Corbett sat on the large leather couch, leaning forward, reading the newspaper that was open on the coffee table. Her small Miniature Pinscher, Smudge, was lying on his back, his tiny legs splayed in all directions as he snoozed on her lap.

She glanced toward the stairs as she heard Faith descend, only to watch her stop, look panicked, then run back up. Reece sighed heavily, and went back to reading the paper. She'd tried several times to convince her wife that the outfit she had chosen was perfect, but apparently, based on

Reece's facial expression, the outfits in question were either too frumpy, slutty, or too plain. Reece had no idea she could say so much by simply looking at her lover. She honestly didn't think she conveyed anything other than sincerity. Faith's choices were all okay with her.

Reece sighed once again and prepared herself for her hyperventilating wife as she came down the stairs.

"Okay, tell me the truth."

Reece kept her face as neutral as she could. "I think you look fine."

Green eyes widened in horror. "I knew the skirt was too short!" she yelled.

Reece threw her hands up in defeat and stood, knocking the small dog to the floor. "Sorry, little man, but your mommy needs attention." She reached out to her retreating wife. "Faith."

Faith spun around and stared at her.

"You need to breathe. Now, come here," Reece insisted, wrapping her arms around the smaller woman. "This is not like you. Where is my strong independent wife? Just close your eyes and breathe."

†

Faith leaned into Reece who began rubbing tiny soothing circles on the small of her back.

"Hon, you look fine."

"Then why'd your eyebrow go up? Why'd you grin like that?"

Reece furrowed her brows. She'd done all that?

"You looked at me with that...hungry look," Faith mumbled into Reece's chest.

"Shit, Faith, in my eyes, you always look sexy. I can't help it. You'd look edible in a paper bag."

Faith snorted. "Thank you, baby," she said with light sarcasm.

"Well, it's true!" Reece defended herself. She pulled away and nudged Faith's forehead with her chin. "Look at me, babe." Green eyes met sincere blue. "I mean it. To me, you'll always be sexy and desirable. I can't fake that you're not. I think you looked fine in every outfit you showed me this morning. Honestly."

"I'm sorry, Reece, I'm being a terrible pain in the ass. I'm so nervous."

"You have every right to be. I could never do what you do. You have guts."

"Oh, Reece, that's so sweet!" Faith laid her head against her lover's chest and wallowed in the strong embrace. Reece was trying so hard, and doing so well for being out of her element. "I love you for being so patient with me. I know I must be driving you crazy."

Reece kissed the top of Faith's head. "Go on, you're going to be late." She reluctantly released her hold. "Are you sure you don't want me to come with you? You know... for support?"

"Oh, honey, you'd be cooped up in a room full of people, or stuck in the car for hours. Not to mention you've become the great Reece Corbett, the wife of that lesbian actress. You'd never last. Thank you for offering again though."

"Well, then, give me a kiss and be on your way."

Faith drew closer and stopped short of the kiss. "The lipstick, Reece."

Reece stuck out her tongue and Faith's tongue met hers halfway. The two rubbed tongues much like Eskimos rub noses.

"Mmm, you better go before I don't let you," Reece purred.

Faith fanned herself. "Whew, don't even start," she warned before turning on her heel and leaving.

†

Reece wanted to sleep, and she knew she should, since Faith would be gone for the duration of the day, but she was too tense. She didn't think she'd be nervous and actually wasn't until she'd lain down and closed her eyes. She began drifting off, but as soon as she got to that point of blissful sleep, she'd jump up. This was foreign to her, and frightening. Rarely had she been scared of anything.

She was discovering a whole world of new emotions since she'd met Faith. She yawned, but knew it was for nothing—there was no fighting it any more. Just as she'd get comfortable, her heart would once again begin to beat rapidly. She sat up in bed. "Shit, I gotta get a grip! You'd think that I was the one auditioning."

She turned to complain to Smudge, but he was more interested in sleeping.

Actually, Reece wished there was someone there with Faith for support. Brad had mentioned hiring a personal assistant to handle Faith's appointments and fan mail, but Faith nixed the idea. She insisted that Reece was all she needed. Reece had smiled at Faith's reaction. After all, she didn't want any lackey following her wife around all day either. However, at this moment, Reece did want someone there, to sit with Faith, at least.

After trudging downstairs and staring blankly into the open refrigerator a while, Reece decided that the only logical thing for her to do was to hit the gym. Upstairs, she changed into sweats and sneakers, and inspected the length of her hair. It was long enough for a ponytail, but one that would stick off the back of her head and look stupid, so she opted instead for her favorite baseball cap. After putting the old, frayed hat on, she kissed the still sleeping dog and left.

Chapter Two

Cori had paced her house like a maniac for most of the morning. She'd promised Faith that she wouldn't go crazy with nerves for her, but she couldn't keep her word. She was so frantic with worry for her friend that she could hardly think of anything else. She hoped Faith would call soon and give her an idea of what was going on.

Cori had total confidence that her friend was going to get the part—she was a stunning actress—but she still couldn't help feeling empathetic for what Faith was probably going through.

"God, she must be a wreck! All alone in that room, surrounded by those primped and preened, pretentious butt-wipes," she said aloud.

Cori paced from the bedroom to the kitchen and back again. "Come on, Faith, call me."

She groaned and flopped down on the bed, spreading herself out face down. "Heh," she said as she giggled. "It smells like my woman." It kept her distracted for a while.

†

Reece was full of nervous energy, so her workout was intense. She had stripped down to a half-shirt and Lycra shorts and still, the sweat continued to spill.

Once upon a time, Reece had never noticed the women who stared at her as she worked out but since Cori had clued her in on it, she now made an effort to be less showy. Cori made it a point to tell her how little Faith would appreciate the other women drooling and occasionally requesting a flex. So Reece put the shoe on the other foot for a change and decided that if any woman, or man, was to look at Faith in such a way, she'd most likely rip their eyes out.

Reece started working out during off hours, and wearing baggy sweats. She actually enjoyed the heavy clothes as they made her sweat more, burning more calories and body fat. Soon enough, Reece was in peak condition, and loving the way she looked. Faith appreciated Reece's body, too, and proceeded to show her how much by worshipping it every chance she got.

Today though, Reece was hyperactive, and the clothes felt like they weighed a ton. She felt as though she hadn't been able to breathe. She had ditched the sweats and now relished the cool air as it hit her over-heated skin. Several others also enjoyed the effects of the cool air on her flesh and openly stared.

Reece decided that a little show couldn't hurt too much. She strode to the squat machine and winked at a small Spanish woman. She stifled a chuckle when the woman blushed. *Oh, yeah, Corbett, you still got it.* As she dropped into her first squat, a group of three women stared wide-eyed. By her fourth squat several more gawking women and men had arrived.

The owner of the gym just happened to pop by at this particular time and seemed curious as to the small crowd that had formed. Reece noticed the suit and smirked to herself. Nothing like showing off to the lesser sex, she always said. She stood up taller and straighter as he approached.

"Hi, I'm Jeff. Pleased to meet you."

Reece eyed the extended hand. *My, isn't he a bit brave?*

"Yes, well." He put his hand in his pants pocket. "I was just watching you and I must admit I was pretty impressed with what I saw."

Reece ducked her head slightly and flashed him a half smile.

"Oh, forgive me, you don't have a clue who I am." He chuckled nervously. "I own this gym and I was just wondering if you're a pro."

Reece raised an eyebrow. "Nope."

"No?" he asked in disbelief. "Well, then, are you interested in a job here?"

Reece pursed her lips and cocked her head, as if seeming to consider it. She glanced at his hopeful face. "What kind of a job?" she asked in a bored tone. Reece Corbett was very happy with her club, and her life, and wasn't about to change anything, but a little play time was always fun.

"A personal trainer. We'd love to have someone like you on the staff," he said enthusiastically.

"Well, I don't know. I'd have to think about it." Reece replied as her cell phone rang.

"Let me leave you my number...."

Reece held up her hand to cut him off as she answered her phone. "Hi, hon. Really! Oh, wow, that sucks. Oh, babe, before you go any further, Jeff here wants me to work as a personal trainer at the gym." Pause. "Yes, I'll have to wear my gym clothes." Pause.

Reece took the phone away from her ear so she wouldn't go deaf. Everyone could hear Faith screaming and Reece was a bit surprised that her wife had it in her to be heard even above the piped in music. Putting the phone back to her ear, she smiled and chuckled as Faith went on about the detriments of showing off Reece's fine assets to a bunch of drooling airheads who just may not resist the urge to touch and then Faith would have to pull their fingers out.

"Okay, hon', hang on a sec," Reece turned to Jeff and shrugged. "My wife won't let me," she said with a devastating smile.

Jeff bit back his shock. "Oh, okay. Maybe she'll reconsider?"

10

"I'll work on it, but I'm not promising anything. She has me on a pretty short leash."

†

Faith took in the various women in the room, some known, most unknown. There were so many of them and Faith was overwhelmed. It was wall-to-wall women of all shapes and sizes. She knew she probably had one thing on all of them—she was openly gay. She went to the sign-in desk and saw more than twenty names listed. No longer nervous at all, she became annoyed, signed her name, and walked out the door. She leaned on the wall outside and calmed down. She was angry that this whole thing had turned into a circus. She tried Reece at home, and when she didn't answer, Faith tried her wife's cell and was infinitely relieved to hear her voice. She calmed immediately and her whole body went limp. That was until Reece mentioned a job at the gym. Then Faith lost her cool completely. All of her pent up anxiety came out in her emphatic tirade against Reece showing off her body. Feeling much better and a little guilty for losing her temper, she groaned into the phone.

"Oooh, honey, you know what that sound does to me," Reece purred, trying to lighten the mood.

"I am a wreck, Reece. I'm sorry I behaved like a lunatic."

"Oh no, don't apologize, I really didn't want to work here anyway. It was a riot though, to see his face when I told him you wouldn't let me." Reece chuckled.

Faith smiled in response. "Baby, I was wrong, I need you."

Reece's stomach dropped. "I knew it! I should have been there with you. Fuck!!"

"No, honey. Calm down. I miss you, that's all. Now that I hear your voice, I'm so much calmer," Faith explained.

"I still say I should have been there with you. You're upset and I'm not there."

Faith smiled. She could practically see Reece's pout. Reece's voice was doing almost as much as one of her hugs would. "It's really all right, I swear. Don't work yourself up about it."

"Okay." She took a few calming breaths. "Would it be a bad thing if I came to pick you up?"

Faith hummed in pleasure. "Oh no, that would be a very good thing. I'm starved."

"About when, do you think?"

Faith glanced at her watch. "A few more hours, but I'll wait for you either way."

"Okay, babe, good luck. I know you'll be just fine.

"Thank you. I love you. I feel so much better now."

"Love you, too. Break a leg or whatever you're supposed to break."

†

Cori couldn't stand it another minute. She called Reece to find out what was happening with Faith's audition and Reece informed her that she was naked and going into the shower. Cori feigned a swoon, told her she'd be right over and hung up before Reece could protest. She let herself in and plopped into her favorite recliner with Smudge. She was waiting anxiously and when the water stopped and Reece didn't appear soon enough for her, she went up in search of her. She stopped at the top of the stairs and stared at Reece's nakedness.

"I didn't expect you to come up," Reece said.

"Christ, Reece, does Faith realize how fucking perfect you are?" Cori leaned against a wall.

Reece chuckled, turned her back on the dancer, and flexed. She laughed as she heard Cori slide down the wall. "May I get dressed now?"

"Please," Cori squeaked.

Reece walked naked into the bedroom and closed the door behind her. Cori hid her face in her hands in disgust. "That is so sick. She's like your sister-in-law."

When Reece emerged, Cori was no longer on the floor so she went downstairs to find her. "That better be coffee I smell."

"You're damned right." Cori met her in the living room with two mugs and gave one to Reece. "So what's happening? Tell me!"

"She's pissed. The place is wall-to-wall beauty queens and she's feeling a bit annoyed. "

"Why are there so many people?"

Reece shrugged and frowned. "Beats me. I'm going to pick her up in a few. By then she should be near hysterical."

"Shit, Reece! I hate that she's going through this. It's gotten so out of control. The damned part was written for her," Cori said angrily.

"I know that, and you know that, but those actresses in there all think they have a shot. That's what's making Faith so pissed."

"I can imagine. Hey, let me come with you?" Cori suggested hopefully.

"Well, I don't know. I was kinda hoping to ease Faith's tension in my own special way," Reece said.

"Oh, come on! You guys should be past that honeymoon stage. Where the hell does lesbian bed death fit into your lives? There will be plenty of time for screwing later. I think she needs a massage, not an orgasm."

"One can never go wrong with an orgasm, Cor."

"Put it away, Romeo. Finish your coffee so we can get going."

Chapter Three

Faith finally entered the office, still annoyed and tense.

"Are you nervous, Ms. Ashford?" A kind looking gentleman asked.

"No, just angry, hot, and annoyed."

The man grinned. "My name is Harry Wells, and I am running the audition process. I have to admit, I was surprised to see your name on the roster. You do realize this part is already yours, don't you?"

"That's what I was told, but after sitting in that room–"

Mr. Wells, cut her off with a smile and a raised hand. "I understand completely. This has gotten way out of hand. We'll contact you with the details very soon." He followed his words with a warm smile.

"That's it? It's finished?" the actress asked in disbelief.

"We'll read a few more women, make a show of it, but yes, that's it."

"Oh, my God. I was just tortured for no reason? I'm going to *kill* Brad!"

Harry smiled warmly. "You have every right to be pissed, Ms. Ashford. I know this was unexpected but we had no choice but to placate the others. I assure you, Bill was adamant about it. He is quite fascinated by you."

Faith blushed, and she wasn't sure why. She recalled that Bill was the only man at the cocktail party on Valentine's Day that wasn't speaking directly to her chest. She chuckled with relief. "You just never know, Mr. Wells. Bill could have been schmoozing like the rest of them."

"Yes, he could have, but you see it's the truth. As soon as we have something halfway decent for you to read, we'll send it to you. Just leave your information with me and you can go take a well-deserved nap." He grinned, seeing her relief.

"Thank you so much!" Faith quickly wrote her information on the offered paper.

"One question." Harry bit his lip worriedly. "Is your partner okay with the intimacy required in this film?"

Faith swallowed hard. "Uh, sure...no problem." She smiled weakly.

Mr. Wells grinned knowingly and laughed. "Haven't told her yet, have you?"

"Heh, well... don't you worry. She'll be fine," Faith replied with an air of false confidence.

"Great!" Harry offered her his hand. "So glad to have finally met you."

Faith took his hand. "Feeling's mutual, Mr. Wells. You made my day. Thank you again!"

†

Cori leaned against Reece's small car, watching as its owner paced the streets. Every time the door opened to the building, Reece's head whipped up and she looked like an expectant puppy waiting for its master. Her shoulders were tense and her jaw muscles were working a mile a minute, making Cori think that Reece was going to need an aspirin soon.

Finally, the door opened and out popped Faith, looking a bit frazzled but grinning widely. Reece took several long strides to get to her and when she did, she was all eyebrows. "Well? What happened?"

"I got it! It's mine!" Faith exclaimed loudly, full of excitement.

Reece picked up the smaller woman and spun her around. Seeing this, Cori bolted toward them and jumped up and down in a circle around the two women. People walking by gave the trio aggravated stares, not because it was unusual to see such a scene in New York City, but because they were blocking a perfectly good sidewalk.

"Yes!" Cori cheered. "I knew everything was going to be fine!"

"No, you didn't. You were a nervous wreck," Reece argued.

"Oh, yeah, right, said she of the dark circles." Cori pointed to Reece's eyes.

"Shut up, freak."

"Both of you shut up." Faith narrowed her eyes playfully at Reece, who returned the favor. "Reece, put me down."

"Kiss me first," she demanded. "And never mind the lipstick."

Faith grinned as she lowered her head. She liked occasionally being taller than Reece, and took advantage of her position by laying a hot kiss on her wife.

Reece swayed a bit then licked her lips. "Mmm, Revlon, my favorite," she joked, then put Faith down as promised.

"Are you guys done yet? I'm hungry," Cori complained.

"You're just jealous. When's Vi getting back, anyway?" Reece asked, leading Faith to the car.

"Tomorrow. What the hell do you do at a piercing convention? I mean, what can she see that she hasn't already? I swear that woman is twisted. You have no idea the things she's stuck through people's parts."

Reece grimaced and then raised an eyebrow as Faith's stomach growled loudly. "That's quite enough, Cor. Let's take my woman out to celebrate. Where do you want to go, babe?"

Faith pulled Reece's arms around her body and leaned happily into her. "Hmmm, I dunno." She shrugged. "Little Italy?"

"Done." Reece nodded disengaging herself from her wife. She opened the car door and ushered Cori in, then Faith. After she climbed into the small car, she leaned and dropped a quick kiss on Faith's cheek. "I knew you'd be all right."

"Thank you for believing in me, baby." Faith smiled brightly, her hand resting on Reece's thigh.

"Yeah, yeah, she's the wind beneath your wings. Can we go eat now?"

Reece glared at Cori in the rear view mirror and peeled out.

†

After eating like pigs and dropping Cori off at her place, the couple headed home themselves. Faith, exhausted from expending all that nervous energy and not sleeping much the night before couldn't wait to get into a hot bath. Reece was more than eager to accommodate. When she offered to add bubbles to the hot tub, she received a face full of kisses.

"I should pamper you more often," Reece teased.

"Please, honey, if you pamper me any more than you already do, I'll become a brat."

"You're already a brat," Reece joked, bending above the tub. She growled when Faith fondled her ass. "I thought you were too tired for that kind of celebration." She threw a sultry look over her shoulder.

"Mmm, look at me like that again and I just may find the energy," Faith purred.

Reece stopped what she was doing, narrowed her eyes, licked her lips, and gave Faith a very seductive look.

Faith shivered. "Oh, yeah, that's the look I was talking about."

Reece pulled open her button-fly jeans with one tug and slowly removed them. "Get in the tub, babe," she said in a low voice.

The actress ran her hands up the front of her body, making sure to dwell on her breasts, just to stir Reece. She stepped into the tub, turned her back to her lover, and sat down slowly, groaning in delight. Reece climbed in behind her, slowly sliding her body down Faith's back. She pulled the smaller woman into her arms and closed her eyes in pleasure, relishing the feeling of their skin touching.

"Oh, Reece," Faith sighed. "This feels delicious. I love it when we sit like this."

Reece dipped her dark head and placed a soft kiss on Faith's ear. "Why do you like it?" she asked in a deep whisper.

"I feel so safe, yet completely at your mercy."

"Quite the contradiction, don't ya think?" Reece teased.

Faith stretched her legs and leaned her full weight into her lover, laying her head back. "I love feeling you around me," she whispered, holding Reece's bent knees against her sides. "I can feel your heart beating."

Reece kissed Faith's shoulder, inhaling deeply. "Have I told you I love the way you smell?"

"Mmm hmm," Faith hummed, covering Reece's hand with her own and moving it to her breast.

Reece grinned, palming her wife's breast. "Someone wants some attention, hmm?"

"That would be nice," Faith purred, pressing Reece's hand firmly.

Reece licked a hot trail from Faith's shoulder to her ear where she sucked the earlobe into her mouth.

"Mmm, baby...make love to me," Faith whispered.

"Your wish is my command," Reece breathed into the soft ear.

She toyed with Faith's nipple, tweaking and rolling it between her fingers. Her free hand tickled its way across the smaller woman's stomach and settled on her thigh. A low groan bubbled up from Faith's chest, causing Reece to groan in return.

Faith tilted her chin up, and licked her lips. "I need you, baby," she breathed, her wet lips teasing Reece.

Reece's hand left Faith's breast and she cupped her wife's chin, tilting her head farther up so their lips could meet. She teased the soft pink lips with her tongue until Faith whimpered and then she slid her other hand lower. She plunged her tongue into Faith's mouth as she slid two fingers through the heated folds below the water. Faith's hips bucked and she groaned loudly into Reece's mouth. She bent her legs at the knees and opened them as wide as she could, inviting more. Reece kept her legs firm, not allowing Faith to open hers as wide as she wanted. This caused her wife to whimper as Reece's long fingers teased her. Reece caught Faith's bottom lip in her teeth and pulled, mumbling around it. "Slow, Faith, slow and long."

Faith moaned. If she couldn't open her legs, she wasn't going to get the amount of pleasure she craved, and it *was* going to be slow and long. "Quick first, baby?" she asked against her lover's teasing lips.

"Uh, uh." Reece slid her mouth along Faith's chin, tasting all the way down to where her neck met her shoulder. "Slooooow," she drawled before sucking the sensitive skin possessively.

Faith grunted in half-protest, and wiggled her hips, attempting to force Reece's touch. She used her hand to press the larger hand more firmly but Reece was much stronger and resisted. "Please, baby?" she begged.

"Mmm, you know how much I love that," Reece said in a low, sexy timbre. Hearing Faith beg always made her sex clench. "It gets me so hot to hear you plead."

"Oh, honey, I just want you so badly," Faith whined, rolling her hips.

Reece adjusted the pressure of her touch as her lover rose to meet her hand. She denied the contact Faith ached for, instead continuing with long, slow, light caresses. She used one finger only, sliding it up the length of her wife's sex. When she reached her clit, she waited for Faith to buck, then slid it down slowly, toying with her opening. Faith kept trying to force Reece's hand, and Reece grinned evilly. "No, baby," she whispered, reaching up and tracing Faith's open lips with her finger.

Faith arched her back at the loss of contact. "Reece..." she whimpered, reaching up and pinching her own nipples.

"Oh, yeah, that's so nice...so hot," Reece said of the view. She rocked her hips, seeking her own relief against Faith's body. "Yeah."

Faith closed her eyes and focused on Reece, and where their skin met. It almost felt too hot where they touched, the heat of the hot water magnifying the sensation. The actress swallowed hard as Reece's pubic hair ground into her lower back. She tried to focus hard enough to imagine where her lover's clit touched her, but Reece began pulling at her nipple ring, erasing all thought except for pleasure. Reece tugged and twisted the ring, and Faith arched her back. "Baby," she moaned.

Reece stroked Faith's sex slowly, in contrast to the rough way she was treating her nipples. Faith was squirming, begging and arching and Reece's heart pounded at the display. Her clit ached for more focused attention, but for now, the friction of Faith's skin would have to do. Trying to put her own need aside, she parted Faith's flesh with two strong fingers and slowly eased the tips inside. Faith groaned loudly and Reece gasped at how tightly her wife's muscles held her fingers. She resisted her intense urge to plunge them in, and instead slipped them out, then in again even slower than before, this time spreading them open.

Faith whined loudly in frustration when her lover's fingers slid out, then cried out in pleasure as they began to penetrate her again, stretching her as they did. "Yes, baby! Fuck me, Reece, please."

Reece's nostrils flared. "Faith," she growled as her lover's hands wrapped around her forearm and wrist, the short nails biting her flesh. "I'm gonna fuck you, all right," Reece promised, her voice a husky purr.

"Yes...please," Faith whimpered, pulling at Reece's arm.

Reece thrust deeply, rubbing her palm into her lover's clit. Faith surged up, her inner walls squeezing the long fingers, keeping them firmly inside. She held the well-muscled forearm tightly, grinding herself into Reece's hand. "Fuck, Reece...yes!" she gasped, her voice hoarse with pleasure.

"You feel so tight and hot," Reece said wiggling her trapped fingers, eliciting a groan from her wife. "Do you want me to fuck you hard?" she asked, then bit Faith on the neck.

Faith writhed as the sharp teeth caught her tender skin. "Oh, yes... fast and hard, please," she begged, gripping Reece's arm tighter.

"Let go, baby," Reece whispered, licking the spot she'd just bit. "Hold on to the tub for me."

Faith whimpered, knowing what was to come. She obeyed her lover and panted in anticipation. A large strong hand wrapped around her throat at the same time Reece plunged inside her. She cried out, slamming her head into Reece's shoulder.

Reece grunted through her teeth and tightened her grip on Faith's throat. She bent her neck, resting her cheek on the blond's head, feeling the sounds of pleasure as well as hearing them.

Faith bucked with the force Reece was using, the water sloshing around and over the sides of the tub. She wanted more. She wished Reece had more hands to touch her everywhere at once. Suddenly, Reece opened her knees, allowing Faith to do the same.

"God, Reece!" she cried.

Reece sunk her teeth into Faith's shoulder, plunging her long fingers in to the hilt, crushing her palm against her lover's hard clit. Faith let go of the tub, and grasped Reece's knees, trying to force them open wider, wanting more of Reece inside of her.

"You gonna come for me?"

Reece's voice was deep and throaty, expressing how turned on she was, and Faith shivered. "Yes, don't move..." she gasped, thrusting hard onto her lover's hand. "Oh, God...oh, God."

Reece's upper lip curled and she could feel her own body tightening in response. "That's right...you come for me."

Faith thrashed in the water, her legs clamping shut on Reece's arm as her orgasm struck her. She groaned and shuddered, her nails digging into Reece's thighs. Reece watched Faith through heavy lids, her own hips jerking. Faith began to relax, and reached behind her, pulling Reece's head toward her own.

They kissed slowly, tongues meeting sensuously, softly, and they stayed entwined until Faith finally fell back heavily. Reece removed her fingers from her lover and slid her hand between them. Faith tried to turn herself around but Reece held her in place.

"You just sit there, this won't take a minute." She buried her face in Faith's neck and touched herself.

Faith wanted to protest harder, but she was spent, and Reece knew that. Faith smiled and reached behind her head, tangling her fingers in wet black hair. She hummed, feeling Reece's hand moving behind her. "Does it feel good?" she asked, playfully.

"Yeah," Reece replied in a tight voice. She felt Faith arch, and knew it was for her pleasure. She lifted her head and glanced down the front of Faith's body to see her perfect breasts bobbing half in and out of the water. "You are so fucking hot," she commented, her voice husky. She reached for Faith's chin and turned her head. "Kiss me when I come."

Faith turned herself sideways and obliged. Reece was right, a few seconds after their lips met, Reece trembled and stiffened. Faith placed her hand over Reece's to be as close to her as she could. She swallowed her lover's grunts, feeling as satisfied as Reece just from holding her. When Reece's hand ceased its movement, she let go of it and embraced her, holding her close. "I love you so much," she breathed into the warm skin of Reece's neck.

Reece held Faith reverently. "I love you, too."

Chapter Four

Faith stretched and yawned, testing her leg muscles after a night of intense usage. Feeling confident that she could walk, she swung her legs off the bed. Smudge twitched his ears, yawned, and stretched all his little legs before curling back up against Reece's head. The high-pitched sound he created with his yawn caused Reece to stir. She slid open an eye and saw Faith about to leave the bed.

"Ugh, mmm," she grunted, reaching out for her wife. Faith was too far away so her arm fell heavily on the bed and she sighed.

Faith turned her head and smiled at the half open blue eye watching her. "Go back to sleep, honey, you don't need to be up."

"You either," Reece complained, patting the bed with her hand.

Unhappy with all the activity, Smudge kicked Reece in the head and harrumphed, licking his lips several times.

Faith scratched the small dog and shook her head. "You two belong together," she commented with a giggle and headed toward the bathroom.

Reece watched dejectedly as her wife's naked butt left the room. "Ain't she something?" she asked the dog, whose tail wagged a couple of times against her ear. After hearing the toilet flush and the water run, Reece waited impatiently for Faith to return. When that didn't happen, she grumbled and tossed the covers off. She pouted at the empty bed, debating whether to go back to sleep or follow her wife. Eventually, she sat up, causing Smudge to slide off the pillow and land on the bed with a whine.

"Sorry, little man, I need to find mommy." She pulled on a pair of boxers and brought the dog with her.

Faith was standing at the kitchen sink filling up the coffee pot, her hair askew and her bare feet poking from the bottom of Reece's bathrobe. Reece grunted inaudibly and wrapped her arms the smaller woman. "Why aren't you in bed?" she managed to ask.

"I can't sleep. I'm too excited about the movie." She walked to the coffee maker, with Reece still wrapped around her. "Why are you so mushy this morning?"

Reece shrugged, knowing not to answer that question for fear of an argument. She knew with this movie coming up fast, Faith's time with her would be limited at best, and she didn't want to face it just yet. "Want me to let go?"

"No, as long as you don't mind me sitting on your lap."

"When have I ever minded that?" Reece asked with a chuckle. "Sooo, you're excited?"

"Yeah!" Faith spun around in Reece's arms and noticed she was topless. She grinned and kissed the bare shoulder in front of her. "This is my movie, Reece! I know the last one was sorta mine, too, but this one is really mine! I star in it! Oh, my God!"

Reece smiled and hugged Faith to her, blue eyes displaying worry as she spoke. "I know, I'm really proud of you, babe."

They stood like that for a while as the coffee brewed. Reece was excited, too, but nervous. Faith was already highly recognized for her last movie and for the TV show and Reece was worried about her being too well known. The paparazzi were already annoying, and soon they'd become a menace. She wasn't jealous, just apprehensive about what might happen to their lives. Faith was a great actress, and should be recognized for her talents, but this was going to stir controversy, big time. They wouldn't get a moment's peace. Reece was already famous by association, and that didn't sit well with her, even now. She couldn't fathom what it would be like after this movie. Suddenly getting anxious, Reece shook her head, and tried to dislodge the negativity. This was very important and exciting for Faith, and she had some nerve feeling the way she did. She chastised herself and focused on her wife as she turned back around in her arms to pour coffee.

They eventually wound up sitting across from one another at the table, drinking their coffee, both lost in thought. Reece was back to her worrisome musings and Faith deep in an entirely different train of thought.

"Why don't we pierce your nipple?"

Reece's eyebrows shot up and she looked down at her bare chest. Her nipples began tightening in fright. "What?"

"Yeah." Faith stared appreciatively at Reece's left breast. "That one. I think it would look great, besides, I'd love to play with it."

Reece's eyebrows never lowered. "Faith, I'm not piercing my nipple." She covered her breast with one hand and winced.

"Why not? You think mine is so hot, well...I think on you it would be hot, too." Faith opened the robe and exposed her pierced nipple. "Look." Reece did, and her lips curled into a sexy grin. "See? All you do is look at it and you get evil."

"Bring that right here," she ordered with a leer.

Faith straddled Reece's lap and narrowed her eyes playfully. "Hmph. Don't think I didn't notice the distraction. I still think we should."

Reece palmed her lover's breasts with both hands and hummed happily.

"You just can't get enough," Faith teased, arching her back into the touch.

"Never. I always want you, now, gimme those lips."

Just as their mouths touched, the phone rang. Reece growled as Faith jumped up to answer it. "Let it ring, for shit sake," she complained.

"Could be Mr. Wells!" she said as she grabbed the handset. "Hello?"

"Hey, you sexy piece of flesh. Are you still fucking?"

Faith giggled. "No, Cor, we were just going to make out."

"Well, quit it, we're coming in."

With that the phone went dead and a key entered the front door lock.

"I'm topless," Reece called out half-heartedly.

"Reece! Go get a shirt on!" Faith ordered.

The brunette rolled her eyes, snatched Smudge up from the floor, and grumbled as she obeyed. She complained as she passed Cori and Violet, "Can't even walk around naked in my own damned house."

"Good to see you, too," Violet replied sarcastically.

Faith hugged the piercer excitedly. "How was the convention? Did you do anything sick?"

Cori reached and yanked down the top of Violet's shirt, exposing her boob. "Have a gander at that!"

Faith's eyes went wide. "Wow!" Violet had crisscrossing barbells in her nipple. "How the hell do you get both in there?"

"Carefully," Violet replied with a wink.

Reece returned just in time to witness this. "What the fuck? I have to go get a goddamned shirt on and she's got her shit hanging out?"

"Calm your drawers, Conan. It was a wardrobe malfunction," Cori said pulling Violet's shirt back up. "I wasn't so thrilled to know my woman whipped her tit out in front of the whole convention, but it is cool."

"Please, Cor, there were ball sacks as far as the eye could see."

The three women made horrified faces.

"Ew! Vi!" Faith exclaimed through a scrunched face. "I prefer my ball sacks of the latex variety."

"Less hair that way," Cori agreed.

"Very pleasant morning talk," Reece said with a disgusted expression.

Smudge struggled in her arm to get to Faith, so she released him to her, grabbed her coffee mug, and headed for the living room.

"Ooo, she's cranky today! Didn't you give her any?"

Faith sighed. "Plenty. She's been brooding a lot lately and I don't know why. She thinks I don't notice, but I do."

"You think it has something to do with the movie?" Cori asked in concern. If Reece was holding something in, it was bound to come out sometime, and in a big way.

"I'm not sure," Faith said with thought. "Anyway, I'll talk to her about it later."

"Speaking of the movie." Violet grinned from ear to ear. "Congratulations are in order! My little Faith, I knew you when." She carefully hugged Faith so not to squash the small dog. "What are we doing to celebrate?"

"Sorry, Charlie, we already celebrated last night," Reece said poking her head into the kitchen.

"Ha, you're so funny." Cori pretended to laugh. "What say we go out and do something freaky!"

"Cor, just you waking up is freaky," Reece commented.

Violet threw a napkin at her. "Butt out, legs, you already celebrated," she said sticking out her tongue.

"Come on, go get dressed. Today's on me," Violet said, dragging Faith toward the stairs.

†

With their women disappearing upstairs, Reece and Cori were alone. Cori stared at Reece inquisitively, following her wherever she went, until Reece couldn't stand it any longer.

"What the fuck is your problem?" she asked in irritation.

Cori laughed, totally expecting the outburst. "I was just gonna ask you that. What's with the face? It's way unattractive."

"What are you, writing a book?" Reece replied, picking up the tiny dog and plopping down into the sofa.

Undeterred, Cori followed. "Maybe. I think I'll call it Stupid Reece and Her Ugly Face." Cori sat cross-legged on the coffee table and watched in amusement as her friend ignored her. Reece had diverted all her attention to Smudge as she petted him and pretended to clean his eyes. Cori rolled her eyes as Reece peeked in his ear.

"Make yourself useful and get me a Q-tip."

Cori blew out a breath and disappeared to the guest bathroom that was right next to the living room. On her way out, she could hear Reece talking to the dog.

"At least I know you won't be spending all your time making a movie, you'll be right here where you should be. Look at that ear, it's got all sorts of crap in it. Cor? You coming or what?"

Cori sighed heavily. She knew what Reece's problem was now, but there was no solution to it. Faith was making this movie, and that came with a lot of extra shit for Reece to deal with, and Reece didn't deal well with shit. Cori sighed again, realizing what Reece would be going through and how difficult she could become. Justifiably difficult. She smiled weakly at how Reece was keeping it to herself, and not making Faith feel guilty, but still was upset because she wasn't going to be able to make her friend feel better. When Cori finally turned the corner into the living room, she laughed out loud at the various ear products Reece had laid out in a row on the coffee table.

"It's about time, what did you do, take a shit while you were in there?"

"Yeah, and I didn't even spray. Here, Miss Impatient." She handed her a bunch of Q-tips and sat down to watch her large, intimidating friend delicately clean the tiny dog's ears.

She smiled at the image, and decided to file it away for recall in the near future when Reece was being unbearable.

"Oh, little man, this is not good, you have a sick ear," Reece said, voice worried.

"Thelma and Louise came down with ear mites from the neighbor's cat. Maybe he has them, too?"

Reece looked horrified. "He does NOT have bugs in his ears!"

Cori chuckled. "They're miniscule, Reece, and he *can* get them."

"*You* must have brought your dogs' bugs to him. Oh, man, now he has to go to the vet! I hate going to the vet! They stick a thermometer the size of a baseball bat up his ass!"

Cori shook her head in amusement. For someone who generated a whole lot of carnage in her life, Reece was incredibly squeamish when it came to her dog. "I'll take him if you want."

"No way, you gave him ear bugs in the first place. I'll take him. I'll take him as soon as Faith and Vi leave for their day of freakishness."

"At least let me come with you. I'll be bored," Cori begged with a lower lip pout.

Reece thought for a second. "Okay, you can come with. At least I'll know what you're up to."

†

Faith and Violet were well on their way to shop but there was an argument when Reece insisted they use the car and driver Reece had hired for Faith. The two women were against it because they wanted to walk. Reece had a loud fit about Faith wandering the streets of New York unattended, but Violet, Faith, and Cori drove her insane with what Reece called their chicken cackling, until she gave up. Now she was crankier than before, worrying about Faith's wellbeing on top of everything else. Finally getting in touch with the vet, the scowling woman walked out the front door.

Cori jumped up from the couch. "Reece! Wait up!"

"You snooze, you lose, get a move on."

Cori jogged out the door to keep up with Reece's long strides. "Jeez, it's not like he has rabies or anything. It's probably just dirt. And I thought Faith told you not to put that monstrous collar on him."

"He doesn't have dirt in his ears. I clean them, you know," Reece replied defensively, shining Smudge's spiked collar with her shirt. "He likes his collar, thank you very much."

Cori laughed out loud and received a menacing look. "Hey, I happen to think it's cute how you obsess about that little eunuch."

"Little man, thank you. Just because Faith and her sadistic needs had to chop his balls off, he's still a man."

"You know, I saw on TV where they have prosthetic testicles for dogs. You can get him Great Dane balls. That way, between that collar and his balls, he'll be totally unable to walk."

Reece turned and growled at the dancer, as they headed through the vet's door.

Reece walked to the front desk and announced her presence to the receptionist, who winced. She remembered the neurotic standing before her from when the small dog was neutered. She hurried to get the chart to avoid any confrontations

"Just have a seat. The doctor will be right with you."

"I'm not waiting forever," Reece complained before her ass even hit the chair.

"God, Reece, you're one of those clients who drive people to drink," Cori observed, lingering by the brochures.

"Bite me."

The doctor's assistant appeared. "Goliath, Goliath Corbett."

Cori's eyes widened. "Goliath?"

"Shut it." Reece stood and followed the assistant.

Cori sat in the waiting room, laughing herself stupid. "Wait till Faith hears that one!" Suddenly she was dragged into an exam room by her ear and she raised an eyebrow at Reece.

"I don't trust you out there."

"You sure you want me to see you swoon when they take his temperature?"

Reece stood taller. "I do not swoon."

Later, Reece stomped out of the vet's office with a big fat scowl, followed by Cori who wore a smug grin. She didn't dare speak to Reece yet. Reece needed time to calm down after what had happened . Turns out, Smudge, aka, Goliath had an ear infection and when the doctor suggested a deep cleaning, with sedation, Reece had a fit, snatching her dog off the table and attempting to flee.

Cori finally convinced her to allow it, talking to her until she understood that this was going to make him better. Unable to hand him to the vet, there was a tug of war of sorts with the tiny dog, the doctor winning. Reece stood, menacing, eyes narrowed, arms folded to emphasize her muscles... as if daring the doctor to hurt the dog. He filled the syringe, stuck the dog with it and Reece's knees promptly buckled.

Now, Cori was dealing with a horrified Reece who was grasping her sleepy dog and racing through the streets with long strides to run away. Cori was getting tired, trying to keep up.

"Reece, please, I won't tell anyone, I swear! Just slow down, will ya?"

"Oh, you know better. Besides, I think it was a sudden sprain," Reece said, red faced, reaching down to rub her knee.

Cori snorted. "Yeah, that's what it was."

†

As soon as Reece settled Smudge at home, the doorbell rang. Peeking out the window she saw it was the FedEx guy and frowned. She had no desire to have the FedEx guy bother her.

"It could be her script, ya know." Cori poked Reece.

"Right." Reece sighed and opened the door.

The delivery guy looked back and forth between both women, then behind them with disappointment. "I'm looking for Faith Ashford?"

Reece took the guy's pen out of his hand. "She's not here. I'll sign for it."

"Oh." The deliveryman looked dejected.

Reece glared at him impatiently as he clutched the box close to himself. "Are you gonna give me that or do I have to take it from you?"

"Well, I was kinda hoping...I mean, Faith Ashford lives here?"

Reece growled and snatched the package away. "Well, I do, and you wouldn't want to piss me off, buddy."

Cori snuck around Reece and sneered as best she could. "Yeah, me neither." She made biting gestures at him.

Reece slammed the door and shook her head. "Great. That's all I need! Fuck!"

"It's not like you won't see him coming. He is wearing orange and blue."

She glared at Cori. "Make yourself useful and call Faith. Tell her the script is here. I have to do something."

Cori raised an eyebrow at Reece. "What do you have to do?"

Reece scooped up the small dog and cleared her throat. "He's sick," she replied in a quiet voice.

"Reece, you're not going to spoil him any more than he already is, are you?"

"Lick me."

†

Cori stuck her tongue out at Reece as she ascended the stairs, then stared at the box. With her excitement building every second, she shook it, and tried to tear a small hole in it. Finally, after nosing as much as she could with no luck, she picked up the phone and dialed Faith.

"Hi, baby!"

"Well, hello, honeylamb."

"Oh, Cor...what's up? Where's Reece?"

"She's busy doing some irreversible damage to the dog. Your script is here! I wanna open it!"

"It's *there*? For real? How big is it?"

"Yep! I'm holding it in my hot little hands right now! It's pretty heavy. Please let me open it!"

"Cor! Behave. I'm sure you'll be there when I do open it."

"But I wanna be special. Pleeeeeeease?"

Faith laughed. "Oh, all right, you big baby, go on and open it. I'm on my way home anyway."

Cori hung up the phone and tore into the box like a kid tearing open candy. It was two big binders full of script. She held it in her hands, pretended to weigh it, smiled and giggled excitedly. Looking around, she saw no sign of Reece and peeked inside. She shuffled through the first binder, then the second. She blinked a few times after thinking she saw the words naked and bed. She thumbed through that particular section of the script again and came upon what she was looking for. Jesse was naked, in bed with Meredith and from the looks of it, it wasn't the first time. Cori's stomach began to drop until she realized she had no idea what character Faith was playing and it very well may not be her at all. Nervously, she read further, liking very much what she saw, but uncomfortable with putting Faith as any of the characters.

Reece stomped back into the room, and Cori slammed the script shut, almost throwing it on the table.

"What the hell?" Reece asked, pointing to the open box.

"Faith said I could!" Cori's voice was high pitched and nervous.

Reece raised an eyebrow and approached the two binders. Cori ran and grabbed them. "Do you think it's respectful to peek at it if she hasn't read it yet?"

"Did you?"

"Me? No! I wouldn't do that!" Cori replied defensively.

"Fine, I'll wait, but just in case." Reece took the script and put it on top of the entertainment center so Cori couldn't reach it.

"I'm hurt that you don't trust me."

"You'll live." Reece handed Smudge to Cori and went to the fridge.

"What the...? Reece, he smells like your cologne!"

"I gave him a bath. He likes the bubbles."

"Oh, Lord. Does Faith know you bathe him in the Jacuzzi?"

"She doesn't have to." Reece glared, getting out chicken leftovers.

Cori watched with interest as Reece pulled the food processor out and started picking chicken off the bones. "You're pureeing chicken?"

"Yes."

"What? Do you have a tooth ache?"

"It's for the little man."

"Oh, brother!" Cori rolled her eyes and kissed Smudge on the nose. "You are so lucky, do you know that Goliath?"

Reece spun around and pointed at Cori. "Oh, and no Goliath in front of Faith."

"Yeah, I saw how fast you whipped that collar off. You are so pussy whipped."

Reece guffawed. "I am not!"

Cori snickered. "Yeah, right, sure."

"I'm sure you know I could kill you with one poke to the neck."

"C'mon, Goliath, let's leave the Terminator to her pureeing."

†

Faith and Violet burst through the door in a flurry of bags and perfume, nearly knocking Reece to the ground.

"Hey!" she shouted, clasping the tiny dog to her chest.

"Where is it?" Faith asked, hurrying through the house.

Cori grabbed her excited friend by the back of the pants and stopped the nonsense. "Settle down, Reece put it away so I wouldn't peek."

Faith snickered. "And I'm sure that worked. Not."

Reece reached up and took the script down, grinning at how wide Faith's eyes became at the size of it.

"Oooo, gimme!"

Reece dropped the heavy script down on the coffee table, and all four women hovered over it, looking at it intently, like it might do a trick. Cori was the first to act and reached for a binder. "I'll read it to you, if you want."

Faith snatched it away with both hands and promptly sat on the other binder. "Oh no, you don't, I bet you already know what happens in scene eighty-five by heart," Faith joked.

"Actually, scene ninety three," Cori mumbled. Violet chuckled, thinking it was a joke and they all huddled around Faith as she opened the book.

"All right! Time to leave my wife alone," Reece ordered, pointing at the door.

"What? No fashion show?" Violet asked, gesturing to a big pink bag. "And I wore panties with ass cheeks just for that reason."

Reece cringed. "I'm sure I don't want to see what's in that bag, anyhow. Come on, Faith's gonna be buried in that script for the rest of the night."

"Thank you, baby," Faith said, already deeply involved in the first pages.

Cori sighed. "Well, all right! Let's go, Vi. I, for one, am dying to see what's in the bag. Love ya, Faith."

"Love you back, Cor, now shoo!"

Reece smiled at Faith's willingness to throw the girls out. "Later. Lots," she said as she held the door open.

Cori blew kisses. "Love you, too, Reece."

"Bite it."

Locking the door behind her, Reece walked slowly toward Faith. The actress, buried in the script, had a look of anticipation on her face. Reece watched her for a minute, then held Smudge at arm's length. "He has an ear infection."

"Mmm."

"It was deep...like to his brain."

"Mmm."

"They gave him a needle, knocked him out. He has medicine."

Faith glanced up for a second and blew Reece a kiss.

Reece's eyes narrowed. *And so it begins.* She squatted down by the coffee table and cleared her throat.

Faith looked up and realized what she was doing. Closing the script, she smiled apologetically. "I'm sorry, baby, I was just excited." She leaned and kissed her wife softly. "What happened today? Tell me all about it."

Confused to find herself actually pouting, Reece stood and turned away from Faith, eventually disappearing as she spoke. "He needs medicine in his ear twice a day and I have to clean it out every three days. The needle was big, really big," she said with little emotion.

Faith felt bad. The last thing she wanted to do was ignore Reece. She got up and followed the sound of her voice into the kitchen.

"Anyway, I'll take care of him. I know you're going to be busy with the script and all—" Reece hesitated when she felt Faith's hands slide around her waist.

"I'm sorry." Faith kissed the middle of her lover's back, and then rested her cheek on it. "Mmm, baby. Forgive me?"

Reece pursed her lips and rolled her eyes. "Yeah, of course I do. I'm being an asshole. I know how much this means to you."

Faith slipped around to the front of her woman and kissed Smudge, then Reece's tattooed arm. "Don't be ridiculous. I ignored you and that's just wrong. I have plenty of time to read that. Tell me about the needle."

Reece cocked her head and smiled. "It wasn't really that big, but compared to him…." She bent down and put the small dog on the floor. "It was a javelin. And don't listen to anything Cori says about it, my knee cramped."

Faith looked quizzically up at her wife. "Your knee cramped? At the vet?"

Reece made a pained expression. "Yeah, just like that, it hurt me and I had to hold onto the table for a second. But it went right away."

Faith looked from the dog, to Reece, to Reece's knee. She grinned knowingly. "Well, it looks like he survived the needle and it looks like you survived your knee." Faith hugged Reece tighter, knowing there were no knee cramps, just a soft spot for Smudge. "Does it hurt now? Do you want me to rub it?"

Reece cleared her throat, already uncomfortable about fibbing to Faith. "Uh, it's fine now, but you can rub anything, anytime." She reached down and squeezed Faith's butt.

Faith smiled deviously. "How about we go upstairs and...She wiggled her eyebrows, then nodded toward the pink bag she brought home from shopping, "A little fashion show, maybe?"

Reece grinned and chuckled. "How many outfits you got in that bag?"

"Three."

Reece picked Faith up, hoisting her over her shoulder. "I say you don't make it to two."

Faith giggled and smacked Reece on the ass. "Oh, but the second one requires you to use teeth..."

Reece took off running.

Chapter Five

Dressed in her signature tuxedo, Reece sat on her usual barstool, lost in thought. The music pounded in the background as patrons vied for a spot at the bar around her and the bartender was doing fancy bottle tricks for tips. Reece wasn't interested. With visions of Faith twirling around in her shiny new purple garters swimming in her head, she sat motionless, a sexy grin on her face as she recalled the scene.

"You like?" the actress had purred, running her hands up the front of her silk covered body.

Reece lounging on the big bed, had eyes riveted on her sexy wife. "Bring that here and I'll show you how much."

Faith crawled onto the bed between Reece's open legs, head thrown back, eyes closed, swaying to a beat only she could hear.

Reece growled and reached out for the seductress.

Faith backed away. "Uh, uh... your teeth, remember?"

Reece got up on all fours and approached her teasing lover. "Ah, but you didn't say where I could use my teeth, did you?"

"Hey, boss lady, what's hangin'?"

Reece's head snapped up and she growled again, but this time it meant an entirely different thing.

Cori snickered. "Oooo, bust a good thought bubble, did I?"

Reece rolled her eyes. "Aren't you supposed to be dancing naked somewhere?"

Cori stretched her arms out and posed. "Just finished. Note the fine sheen of sweat on my glistening body."

"Lovely." Reece averted her eyes to the television above the bar, suddenly straightening up with great interest.

Cori followed her friend's line of vision and her eyes went wide. They both watched, totally rapt, as Shakira writhed around half-naked, gyrating, and humping.

Reece, suddenly feeling shocked, was the first to blink. "For shit sakes! She's inhuman!"

Cori turned her back to the bar. "If the thought police were here, they'd wash my brain out with cleaner." She laughed at Reece's expression. "It's all right, Reece. It's supposed to make you hot."

Reece nodded enthusiastically in agreement and sighed, signaling the bartender for a drink.

Cori pointed at the stage. "Hey! The new girl is gonna dance in a minute! Wanna throw ice at her with me?"

Reece snickered. "Be nice. Cori, you were new once, too."

"Yeah, and they put the ice in my bra and tipped me with Monopoly money," Cori said with narrowed eyes. "Come to think of it, you were the only one who tipped me with a real five."

Reece ducked her head to the side and shrugged. "You were new."

Cori smiled and suddenly hugged her boss. "Awww, you knew they would treat me bad. My hero."

"Cut it out!" Reece shook Cori loose and stood up. "I need to go to my office." She snatched her drink and walked away.

Cori smiled long after she left. Reece never could accept that kind of attention, but Cori knew she deserved it. Funny thing was, Reece didn't think so.

†

In the semi-silence of her office, Reece sat back in her chair and put her feet on the desk. She twirled the straw in her drink absently as she thought about the near future with

Faith. There was nobody more proud of, or happier for Faith right now. However, Reece knew these next long months were going to be hell to endure. Not one for constant attention, and certainly not needy, Reece was endlessly puzzled by her behavior when it came to Faith. She was intelligent, and knew Faith, justifiably, would be buried in this movie, but when she thought about being home all those days without her wife, she felt jealous.

She blew out a frustrated breath and swigged her drink. Why should she feel like that? Faith loved her. She wasn't jealous of her job and she had so many more reasons to be jealous of Reece's job than Reece of hers.

She sat motionless for a while, trying to make sense of her unusual emotional insecurities. This kind of stuff was new to her, and she didn't really like how it made her feel. Her thoughts ran rampant.

I am not needy! I can do just fine when Faith is at work. What do I expect? She can't sit around the house every fucking day without going crazy. Although, that doesn't sound half-bad. No big parties, no photographers chasing us everywhere we go. What the hell am I saying? Shut up. Just shut up. This is Faith's dream and I have no right to feel this way. She never says a word about my line of work, and she could have plenty to say. I'd blow a vein if she were around even one naked woman. She's an actress, I love her. I will deal with it.

Having made a final decision, she stuck out her chin in defiance of the jealousy. She marched right out into the club and decided there was nothing wrong with watching Cori throw ice at the new girl as long as she pretended not to see it.

†

Faith sat back on the couch and blinked rapidly in disbelief. Her heart was racing and her mouth was dry at what she had just read. She threw the script angrily onto the coffee table and held her head in her hands. "How the hell am I going to do this?"

She stood and began pacing, her nerves frazzled, her head swimming. "What am I going to do? How do I tell Reece?" Holding her hand to her forehead, she stopped pacing and stared at the script. "I mean, I guess I knew it would happen... it is a lesbian movie but—" Her hand traveled slowly down her face until it covered her mouth. Wide eyed, she flopped back down on the couch. "Oh, my God...this is bad."

†

Cori closed her locker and started to leave when she noticed several messages on her cell phone, all from Faith. She immediately called back, knowing exactly what it was about.

"Cor?"

52

Faith sounded very tense with just one word.

"Scene ninety-three, huh?"

Faith blew out a loud breath. "Oh, shit, Cori! What am I going to do?"

"Well, according to the script, 'a whole lotta lovin'."

"Gee, thanks, friend." The actress rolled her eyes. "How much of it did you read?"

"Honestly, I just skimmed it really, but I saw enough to know you'll be knockin' boots."

"God! Cori! You should see what I have to do! First of all, I'm topless... second of all, they want all sorts of artsy camera angles and weird shots of me having an orgasm! *Cori!* That's like five takes of me faking an orgasm topless! Can you believe the direction actually says 'perky nipples?' That means there will be ice involved. I've heard the stories... *fuck!*"

Cori winced with every word. "Oh, honey." She really didn't know what to say, this was an independent lesbian film. There was bound to be action in it. "Do you know who plays the other chick?"

"Cori!"

"Sorry, just thought I'd lighten the mood."

Faith sounded panicked. "What am I going to tell Reece?"

"What can you tell her? Tell her exactly what she needs to know."

"Needs to know? Damn! She's not going to like this one bit. She's gonna freak!"

"Maybe. But she'll have to come to her senses. It's just acting." Cori didn't even believe the crap she was saying. Who was she kidding? Reece will have a fit to end all fits, probably destroy everything in sight, have a stroke, and then kill everything with tits on the movie set.

"Cori, this is Reece we're talking about, not Gandhi. She will not be sensible and peaceful. She's gonna lose it and you know it."

"Faith, look—"

"No, you look! I'm scared!"

Cori's eyes widened. "Of Reece? Faith, she'd never hurt you."

"No, not that... I don't think I can do this."

"It's just acting, Faith. You're not actually having sex with the woman, and besides, I'm sure you can talk to the director about the content."

"Yeah, I suppose I can."

"Sure," Cori continued. "They wrote the part for you, you have to have some say."

"But, Cor, what if they won't change it? Maybe I should just forget it. Maybe I should just forget acting altogether. Reece is going to have a major coronary. It may not be worth it."

"Faith Ashford! You did not give up the life of fucking Riley to live in a rat infested, piss smelling tenement to follow a dream, only to throw it away because you think Reece will be unreasonable! Now you stop that shit and stop it now!"

Reece popped her head into the dressing room. "Freak, I'm locking up, light a fire under it, will ya?"

Cori glared at Reece.

"Fine, have it your way." Reece shrugged and walked away.

"Faith, listen, Reece is leaving now. Promise me you'll talk to her when she gets home."

"Okay. I will."

"Good. Now I love you, but your lovely, understanding wife is going to lock me in to starve all night if I don't go now."

†

Reece threw a leg over her Harley and started it up. With a mischievous smile, she revved it several times, delighting in the multitude of car alarms the sound set off. Pepe, the garage attendant, shook his head after the initial fright, and began the task of gathering keys from the hooks. Every so often, Reece would be in a mood and he could do nothing about it. She was a great customer and a fabulous tipper, but honestly, he was a bit afraid of her.

Reece waved and laughed at Pepe as he scrambled all around the garage pressing key chains, shutting off some and setting off new alarms. She was in a playful mood for a change, and even if it lasted one split second, she took advantage of it the best she could at four in the morning. She leaned back and wished she felt Faith behind her. She had an urge to just take off to the country—just the two of them—and leave reality behind. Already anticipating being left alone while Faith filmed, Reece was feeling selfish and wanted to steal Faith away. Knowing she couldn't gave her a twinge of jealousy. So far, for now, it made her want to be with Faith more and more while she had the chance, instead of becoming angry with her. Needing her wife right now, Reece revved the engine once more before peeling out of the garage.

†

Reece thought about Faith the entire way home, hoping that her wife would be awake. Noticing the light on in the window, she excitedly opened the door and was even more pleased to see Faith standing there at the door. "You're up," she said with a smile.

"Yeah." Faith cracked a half smile back. "So, how was work?" she asked nervously.

Reece eyed Faith in her sleep clothes and grinned wolfishly. "Work was fine, but that's not what I want to talk about." She advanced on Faith until she backed her against the arm of the couch.

"Reece…"

Reece covered Faith's lips with her own and wrapped a supportive arm behind her back. "Mmm, I've been waiting all night for this."

Faith couldn't help but feel the effects of such a kiss, but she still needed to talk. "Uhm, baby—"

"Shhh," Reece kissed her wife thoroughly and deeply, lifting her up and laying her on the couch. She kicked off her boots and crawled on top of her. "I want you."

Faith closed her eyes, ran her hands up and down Reece's hard body, and groaned. "But I want to tell you…"

Reece nipped a full lip. "Kiss now, talk later."

Faith's entire body melted into the couch as Reece began a devastating oral attack.

Chapter Six

The next afternoon, Faith was again nervously awaiting the rumble of Reece's Harley, Faith jumped out of her skin when the phone rang. Not wanting to be on the phone when Reece came home, she let the machine pick up. Cori's stern voice did nothing for her anxiety.

"Faith, I know you're there, and I won't hang up until you talk to me."

The actress walked slowly to the phone while Cori hummed the theme from Jeopardy. "What is bad timing, Alex?"

Cori chuckled despite the seriousness of her call. "What exactly did you tell Reece about the script?"

"Not enough. Shit, Cor, this is bad! There are things in this movie I love, but then there are things I don't exactly feel comfortable with."

Cori's eyebrows went up. "Elaborate."

"The story is great. Meredith is a fantastic character, but the sex is just short of the Playboy Channel."

"Well, like I said, they wrote it for you and if you like the rest, you probably have the clout to change the smut factor."

Faith grimaced, at the word smut. "I hope, but in any case, I have to tell Reece and I'm expecting her any minute. I'm just about ready to have a panic attack!"

"I just left her, she should be there any second, and the good news is she's in a pretty cool mood."

Faith's eyes widened. "Really?"

Cori screwed up her face. "Yeah, but then again, I don't know that there's anything that could help break that kind of news to her. Good luck and if you need me, I'll be holding my cell in my hand all night."

Faith grumbled. "Great, now I'm scared again!"

"Aw hon, now, you know she'll blow hard, but after hearing that you aren't comfortable with it and are going to fix it, she'll most likely mellow down a little bit."

"Oh, God, I hope." The sound of the Harley driving up put Faith into full panic mode. "Cori! She's here!"

"Relax! You're gonna be fine!"

Reece walked in just as Faith hung up the phone and she strode across the room to kiss her wife. "Did you finish the script?"

Faith watched silently as Reece went to the kitchen, grabbed a fork, and opened the fridge. She pulled out a container of left-overs and began eating.

"I'm starved," she said between mouthfuls.

Faith, though nervous, decided it was now or never. "Reece, I need to tell you something and you're probably gonna want to put the food down."

Reece raised an eyebrow and stopped chewing. "What's this about?"

"The script."

Reece shoved another forkful into her mouth. "What about it? Don't you like it?" she asked between chews.

"Well..." Faith shifted her feet. "Yes and no."

Reece, getting tired of the stalling, put the food on the table and stared at her wife. "What is it you don't like?"

Faith swallowed hard. "The sex." Her voice was barely audible.

Reece's eyebrow went up and she cocked her head. "The what?" she asked carefully.

"The sex," Faith repeated, with a grimace.

Reece's chest seemed to expand and she lifted her chin. "The sex," she repeated, her jaw clenching tight. "What sex?"

Faith took stock of her extremely tense wife and thought for a moment how to reply. "My character, Meredith, has a love interest, Jesse, and they—"

The fork Reece was holding bent into itself and her nostrils flared. "Really," she said through her teeth. "Are we talking about a kiss... or what, Faith?"

Her wife's barely controlled temper was just about to explode, and Faith couldn't answer this question without fireworks. "Um, naked sex. Reece there's no reason to fly off the handle..."

Reece slammed the bent fork down and gripped the counter with both hands. "No reason to fly off the handle?" she shouted. "My wife is going to be naked on the big screen with another woman, having *sex* and there's no reason for me to fly off the handle?"

Faith winced. Expecting it and seeing it were two different things. "Yeah, but Reece..."

"No, that's fine! I mean it's all in the name of acting, right? How many times do you have sex?"

"Three, but that's not the point..."

Reece stormed around the kitchen waving her arms wildly. "*Three?* Fuck, Faith, *we* don't even have sex three times in two hours!"

"If you just listen to me—"

Reece interrupted Faith again with another tirade. "Wow! Fantastic! Super! This is wonderful! You're going to be fucking some other woman for entertainment! I'm thrilled!"

"*Reece!* Let me finish one goddamned sentence!"

All Reece could see in her mind's eye was Faith naked on a huge screen having sex with a faceless woman. "No, you let me finish! Is that what you really want to do? To me?" She banged on the counter with both fists.

"Excuse me? To you?" Faith yelled.

"What? You didn't think about me? How I would feel?" She shook her head to lose the images. "Did you think I'd be fucking happy for you? Did you think I'd jump up and down? Yay! My wife is gonna have sex with someone else! Yay!"

Although Reece's jumping up and down and clapping was disturbing, Faith was really pissed. Reece wasn't allowing her to get a word in edgewise. "Would you just shut up a second and stop yelling?"

"No, cuz I can't do shit about it! Do you want me to sit here and say with a smile that I'm okay with this? That you are going to be naked in front of a crew of pigs, and some strange woman will be touching you and I'm supposed to stop yelling and smile? Someone else will be smelling your neck, tasting your lips? My stomach burns and my head hurts and I can't do anything about it because it's your life and your movie?" Reece grabbed her stomach and turned away. "I have no say."

Faith's eyes welled up. She walked to her wife and stood inches behind her. Feeling the heat come off her body she wasn't sure if she should touch her. "Baby, I don't want to do it either. I don't want to make you sick."

"Good. Then don't do the fucking movie."

"Reece, you mean more to me than anything, but, I want to do this movie, it's—"

Reece turned seething eyes to Faith. "Fine! Do the fucking movie!" she shouted before storming out of the kitchen.

"Reece! Don't you dare leave! I'm not finished!" The door slammed and Faith screamed out of frustration. "*You never let me finish!*" she yelled, throwing the mangled fork across the kitchen.

†

Cori was already holding her cell phone in anticipation so when it rang she answered it in half a ring. "What happened?" she practically yelled. Violet leaned close to hear the conversation.

Faith, frustrated beyond belief and relieved to hear Cori's voice, burst into tears.

"Honey? Talk to me!" Hysterics was terribly un-Faith-like.

Faith composed herself. "It was awful. She didn't even care what I had to say, she just yelled and yelled."

"Where is she now?" Cori asked, as Violet rubbed her back.

"I have no idea, she slammed out of here a few minutes ago." Faith inspected the wall where the fork hit.

"What did you manage to say to her?"

"All I got out was that there was sex. That was the magic word. After that, she didn't care what I had to say. She didn't let me explain that I didn't want to do the sex either, all she heard was I liked the script and she freaked the hell out."

Cori shook her head. "Oh, man...I knew this was gonna happen."

Violet leaned into the receiver and offered her opinion. "Maybe you should have started at the end first and worked your way to the middle?"

"Guys, I had no idea we couldn't talk like humans. Sure, now that sounds great, but really... who knew she'd cut me off at the knees every time I started to talk?"

Cori closed her eyes and sighed heavily. "She can't handle this. She can't handle the idea of you having sex, even if it's fake, with someone else. My question is, what is she going to do about this?"

"She said her stomach hurt, Cor. She thinks I *want* to do this. It must be killing her." Faith's eyes welled up imagining what Reece was feeling. "Shit, Cor, I hurt her." Faith's voice cracked with tears.

Cori sighed. "I'm coming over."

"No, you have to work. I don't know what happened a minute ago. I'm not exactly the weepy type. I'm okay now. I promise. She'll cool off and I'll be able to talk to her later."

"Faith." Cori rolled her eyes. "Are you sure you want to be alone? I'll bring the alcohol."

Cori could tell Faith smiled, despite her mood. "Nah, really, I'm okay. Reece is in a bad enough mood as it is. If you don't show up for work, she'll freak out on you, too."

"Please. Pshaw. I can take her." She looked to Violet whose eyebrow shot up in disbelief.

"I swear I'm fine. You're the best, Cor. Now get yourself ready for work, you're going to be late. Love you, too, Vi."

Violet grabbed the phone. "Maybe I should come over? Huh? I'll bring Thelma and Louise and we can make it a family affair?"

Faith grinned. "Actually, I have a few phone calls to make. I need to fix this script or I won't be doing this movie. Then I have to think of a way to get Reece to listen to me. Once she's like this…oh, boy."

"Well, okay, but if you need me, you know where I am. I can be there in a second."

"Thanks, Vi, you are both the best."

†

Cori and Violet sat there for a few moments, holding hands. Both of them felt a little helpless not being able to be there to console Faith. Suddenly, Cori jumped up.

"Fucking Reece, I'm going to work and give her a piece of my mind."

Violet held her lover's hand tighter, understanding her anger but not agreeing with running there halfcocked. "Honey, she's already pissed, you have to let her simmer down, or you'll wind up making it worse."

"I'm not afraid of her," Cori declared.

Violet grinned. "I know, baby, but just give her a little while before you start getting in her face. She has to think about this."

Cori stomped her foot. "That's just it! She's not thinking. She won't! She's going to block this out and ignore it and it may destroy them. I won't let that happen."

Violet sighed. "I can't stop you, can I? Okay, just call me if there's any problem."

†

Faith had enough time to relax through her frustrations and started to become angry. She had the phone in her hand several times, ready to tear the filmmaker a new asshole, but knew she had to calm down again before she really created a scandal. It was late, and she knew this guy wouldn't be in the office at this hour and that pissed her off even more. Knowing she had no choice but to wait until morning, she sat and stewed.

She was disappointed in Reece. She thought her wife would have given her enough credit to know she wouldn't do anything to hurt her intentionally. She was angry too, knowing it was going to be hell trying to talk to her about this again without another tantrum.

Smudge, who ran away and hid during all the yelling, came to his mommy and looked at her curiously. Faith picked him up and kissed him on the nose. "I'm sorry for all the yelling, sweetie. Mommy Reece can be a big baby sometimes."

Smudge settled down in Faith's lap and after a while of stroking him, the actress became much calmer. Just as her eyes were getting heavy, the phone rang. She debated picking it up but curiosity got the best of her.

"Oh, Louise! Who's the hot lesbo actress about to make another movie?"

Faith chuckled. "Hi, John. You're a sicko, ya know?"

"I take that as a compliment. Sooo, what's happening? Rumor has it this script is hot!"

Faith groaned. "Hot isn't the word. It's practically porno."

"Huh? Are you serious?"

"Dead serious. John, I'm not going to do it if they don't change it." Faith stuck out her chin as she spoke.

"Oh, wow. What did Spike have to say about it?"

"You don't even want to know." Faith sighed.

"Mmmm. I bet it didn't go over too good," John said sympathetically. "Hey, it's been floating around that Alicia Alvarez got cast, as well. She is a fine specimen, isn't she?"

"Oh, my God! No! Not Alicia!" Faith began to panic.

"What? And here I thought you were a lesbian. Shit, I'd even do her! What do you mean *no*?" John teased.

"I have a huge crush on her and Reece knows it! This is awful!"

John grimaced and covered his tracks. "We don't know what part she's been cast in, so it may not be a disaster.

Besides, she's as straight as a pin and she'd never go for lesbian porn."

"You never know. It's quite chic to be queer; everyone's jumping on the bandwagon. Why should she be any different?"

"Because she's got at least a million boyfriends and is never photographed without one. All are gorgeous, by the way."

"Alicia Alvarez. Fuck. Reece hates her on principle. Says she's a pig."

"Louise, you know Spike is only mad because you think Alicia's the bee's ankles."

"That doesn't make it any better. Oh, man." Faith closed her eyes and took a deep breath. "I'm going to see the producer tomorrow morning, so I'll find out who's playing my love interest. That's if they decide to clean up the script. Otherwise, I'm outta this mess."

†

Cori sat and stewed in the cab, she couldn't believe Reece gave Faith such a hard time. The more she thought about it, the angrier she became at Reece. Finally arriving at the club, she stomped her way up the stairs. Her face fixed in a scowl, she burst into The Lounge full of piss and vinegar.

Sarge was at her usual spot, guarding the door when Cori arrived. The look she gave her let Cori know she was worried about her. "Hey Cor, what's the face for? You almost look as bad as the boss."

"Where's Reece?" Cori asked.

"Somewhere inside. I saw her wandering around earlier. You two arguing or something?"

"Not yet." Cori narrowed her eyes and stormed off in search of Reece. Banging on the office door was fruitless. It was locked and if Reece was in there she wasn't letting on. Pissed, Cori went to the dressing room, with hardly a minute to spare before she was to dance. Angry and frustrated, she changed quickly, made her way to the center stage, and waited for her music to start.

†

The lights went dim, her intro music started, and Cori began to dance seductively. Her foul mood seemed to entice the men and she was picking up tips like crazy. She shimmied to the left side of the stage when something caught her eye. It was Reece, leaning on the smaller stage, with two dancers hanging on her. No wonder Cori couldn't find her, she'd been looking for the tuxedo.

Reece was still dressed in her street clothes, her baseball cap practically hiding her face altogether. Cori saw red as the dancers rubbed themselves on the club owner, touching her sensuously. Reece was eating it all up with a stupid grin on her face. Disregarding her job entirely, Cori jumped off the stage in the middle of her show, and ran to Reece.

Insinuating herself between Reece and a half naked dancer, and shoving the other one away, Cori stood in front of Reece, chest heaving. "What the fuck is your problem?"

Reece tilted her head to the side, an amused expression on her face. "You. I was having a great time until you showed up."

"You are such an asshole, Reece! I don't know what the fuck to do with you!"

A crowd had formed as most of the men watching her perform had followed her when she left the stage. Once people started to realize that she was fighting with the owner, more people crowded around.

Reece towered above the dancer. "How about you just leave me alone and go dance?" She reached out for one of the girls.

Cori exploded. "Fuck you!" She shoved Reece hard. "What the hell are you trying to prove with these girls?" She shoved Reece again.

Reece's eyes flashed and she balled her fists. She clenched her teeth as she spoke. "Get out of my face, Cori, if you know what's good for you."

"No!" Cori pushed Reece again, this time knocking her off balance. "You tell me what the hell you're doing!"

Reece grabbed Cori by the wrist and squeezed. "I...am having fun. At least these girls aren't having sex with me, are they?"

Cori screamed once in frustration. "You suck, Reece. Faith doesn't even want to do that stupid movie and you're an asshole." She wrenched her wrist out of the boss's grasp and stormed off.

"That's only because I don't want her to!" Reece watched Cori as she left. "Yeah, at least I'm not having sex with them," she added.

†

Violet was startled when Cori came flying through the front door. "Honey?"

"That...that...*argh!*" Cori threw herself on the couch and kicked her feet.

Violet stood in front of her. "Honestly, Cor. A tantrum?"

"You have no idea! Reece thinks this is a fucking game or something! She was fucking with the dancers, talking about how she's just having fun, and she's not having sex with them!"

Violet clenched her jaw. "While Faith is at home eating her heart out. That son of a bitch."

Cori flung herself down again. "Tell me about it!"

Violet sat down and rubbed her lover's back. "Why are you home? What happened?"

"I had no choice. Reece probably would have killed me if I'd stayed."

Violet narrowed her eyes suspiciously. "Cori, what did you do?"

"I may have shoved her a few times."

"Cori!"

"In front of everyone," Cori added.

"Have you lost your mind? No, seriously, you shoved her?"

"I was mad!"

Violet sighed. "Okay, looks like no one is thinking rationally but me. I'll be back later."

Cori stood. "Vi! Where are you going?"

"To take care of this the right way, without yelling and scenes. That's the last thing anybody needs right now. And to get to Reece before she does something stupid."

Cori grabbed her lover's hand. "Vi, you can't go there now."

"Watch me."

†

"Okay, show's over." Reece waved her hand at the crowd. "Everything's fine, she's just a little menstrual."

The crowd dissipated slowly and the dancers that were hanging on her seemed to feel awkward after that display until Reece called one back.

The dancer stepped forward and smiled. "Hey, you still up for that lap dance?"

Reece grinned devilishly. "You bet." She sat down on a platform and spread her arms.

I'm right, not doing anything wrong. Fuck that. It's just a lap dance, and I'm not having sex. So what if Cori's pissed? She's just a freak anyway.

The scantily clad dancer shimmied across her but Reece was becoming quite stiff and less relaxed.

I'm not actually touching her. And she's not all the way naked.

Reece took a deep breath and tried to focus on the bare tits in her face. She reached out, grasped the dancer's hips, and frowned.

Fuck, she's bony, nothing to hold on to really.

She let go of the dancer and leaned back.

Her tits are okay, but they're not Faith's. Faiths are perfect and that one isn't pierced and sexy.

Suddenly Reece's stomach hurt again and she felt sick. Scaring the dancer, she bolted up and swiped off her legs. "That's enough," she said curtly and stomped off toward her office.

†

Faith wandered around the house, wishing she could do something right that minute to help diffuse the situation. She wondered how Reece was feeling, how she was handling everything, and what she was doing about it. She wondered also about Alicia Alvarez and if she was really going to play opposite her as a love interest. That would be the hardest to explain, even if she did manage to amend the script's porno quality, there was no way around it. Reece was very aware that Faith had a crush on Alicia. They had talked about it and Reece took an instant dislike toward the woman, even going so far as drawing mustaches and blacking out her teeth on the cover of magazines—even the ones in the supermarket. Faith sighed. She'd never get any sleep with all of this on her mind. Maybe she'd just take Violet up on the offer of company.

†

Cori scowled at the phone as it rang, but answered it anyway. "What."

"Cor? Is that you?"

She relaxed. "Yeah, it's me."

"What happened? Why are you home? Did Reece throw you out?" Faith sounded puzzled and upset.

"No, I walked out. She's probably pissed as hell with me though. Are you okay?"

"I don't know how I feel. I'm up, that's for sure and I'm thinking sleep is not an option. What did you do to Reece?"

Cori snickered. "I may have pushed her."

Faith's eyes widened. "Physically or mentally."

"Physically. Look, I was mad she was being an ass. Anyway, I have nothing to do. Violet went to supposedly put Reece in her place. Want me to come over?"

"You pushed her? Are you crazy? Wait...Violet went to do what? Oh, my God."

"Faith, calm down. If anyone is even tempered, it's Vi."

"If anyone's *not*, it's Reece!'

Cori shook her head. "I couldn't stop her. I'm sure she'll be fine, besides, Reece needs a talking to, and I apparently can't control myself."

"That's it. Maybe I'll go to the club—"

"*No*! Don't...stay there. I'll come over."

†

"Hey, Cori had an argument with Reece and ran out of here about an hour ago. What's going on?" Sarge asked, seeming surprised to see Violet pouncing up the stairs.

"Reece is being a dick."

Sarge winced. "Oh?"

"Yes, and I need to talk to her, where is she?'

The bouncer sighed and pointed. "She's in there somewhere. She told me to stay the hell away from her when I came in tonight and I'm trying my best to do just that. But if you need me, I'm there."

"Love ya, Sarge." Violet kissed the big woman on the cheek.

†

Violet searched all the nooks and crannies of the club and came up empty. She stopped at the bar to get a glass of soda and ventured to Reece's office. She knocked a few times with no reply. "I know you're in there, so you better open this door."

Nothing.

"Reece! Open this door!"

The door opened and a disheveled looking Reece stood there, with the meanest look on her face. "Great. Reinforcements. What do you want?"

Violet walked passed Reece and leaned on the big desk. "We need to talk."

"About what?" Reece asked, annoyance plain in her voice.

"You're fucking up big time, Reece, and you may not get out of this one."

Reece slammed the door and walked in front of Violet. "Oh? Really? Am I getting naked in a room full of sweaty guys and pretending to fuck some bitch?"

Reece's anger was palpable and Vi tried not to flinch at Reece's proximity or throw her soda on her for infuriating her. "Key word, pretending, Reece. You're not a complete fucking moron. It's *acting*."

"That's my *wife*!"

"Yeah, and my wife spreads her fucking pussy for a room full of sweaty guys with hard-ons because they're waving a stinkin' dollar bill at her." Violet sipped her drink calmly.

Reece glared.

"I know you heard me, so don't pretend that you didn't."

She blinked. "That's different and you know it."

"Different? How? She's acting too! Reece, for God's sake, she doesn't want any of those men! She acts like she does and that's why we live in a great apartment in a great neighborhood and have good food on the table! It takes a very clear, well screwed on head to go up on that stage and take her clothes off for money without feeling demeaned or degraded! I'm damned proud of her for it and I tell her every day. When's the last time you told Faith that you're proud of her?"

Reece glowered. "I tell her," she said defensively.

Violet stood tall. "Really? Cuz the way I hear it, you screamed at her and slammed out of the house tonight. She can't be feeling all that great right now and she certainly doesn't think she has your support."

"Violet! She's going to be doing sex scenes!"

"Did you even listen to her? She doesn't want to do those scenes! She hates them! And, she hates that you hate it, too. The last thing she wanted tonight was to have you yell bloody murder and run away. Let me tell you something, if she ever found out what you did with those girls tonight, out of pure spite, I don't think she'd forgive you. I wouldn't."

Reece stepped back. "I didn't do anything with those girls! I was mad, and—anyway, you're not Faith." She folded her arms looking triumphant.

"I wouldn't get so cocky just yet. You have a wife at home, who feels like she disappointed you. You never even let her explain herself. I think you need to go home, and listen for a change. I don't care if you have to dig your nails into your palms, you just shut up and let her talk."

"Are you through, Dr. Phil?"

Violet put her pinky to her lip and thought. "No, there's one more thing."

Reece rolled her eyes.

"You need to apologize."

"Me?"

"Yes, you. And if I were you, I'd make sure it came with flowers. Now, I'm done." Reece was blinking rapidly as Violet waltzed to the door and opened it. "You'll thank me some day."

Reece pursed her lips. "Vi."

Violet turned around, "Yeah?"

Reece got quiet. "I didn't like it, you know. The girls and stuff."

"You don't have to tell me that. I had a feeling you didn't or you wouldn't be locked up in here."

"Uh, what you said...ya know." Reece nodded and pointed to Vi.

"You're welcome." Violet winked and left.

†

Cori and Faith were well through their second pitcher of frozen Margaritas and both felt oodles better for it.

Cori leaned toward Faith and giggled. "So, Alicia Alvarez. God, she's hot."

Faith groaned. "I don't know what I'm going to do. I'll feel like I'm cheating even if it's just pretend."

"That's cuz you're hot for her hoochie." Cori wiggled her eyebrow.

Faith swatted at her. "Stop it!"

"Come on, we all know. Reece knows. You want her booty."

The actress covered her face with her hands. "Oh shit, Cori. I'm totally hot for her booty."

Cori was curious. "Can you kiss her, even though it's acting, and not get hot?"

"I don't know!" Faith panicked. "That's scaring the crap out of me! What if I do get hot? Isn't that cheating? How guilty will I feel?"

Cori smiled. "Hell, I'd do it anyway. How many people can say they tangled tongues with Alicia? A woman no less?"

Faith lit up. "That's right! She's so incredibly straight. She won't be doing anything remotely sexual with another woman. What am I worried about? You think there'll be tongues?"

Cori laughed. "After reading those scenes, I certainly think so."

Faith groaned painfully again. "Anyway, I'm going to take care of this in the morning. If I can help it, there won't be any tongues."

Cori yawned widely. "Speaking of morning, I'm going to crash. I'm done."

"Okay. I suppose I should go to bed, too. I don't want to be up when Reece gets home."

†

Reece sat immobile in her office long after Violet left. She knew Vi was right...about everything. She really hadn't let Faith talk, and now as she replayed the events in her head, she felt a little bit like the asshole Cori told her she was. But apologizing? That was hard. Reece felt she had every right to be angry, Faith was hers and not to be shared. How would Faith like it if Reece decided she wanted to act out a few sex scenes for the world to see?

Reece grimaced. That's pretty much what she did with those dancers not too long ago. It was spite, nothing more than spite. She dropped her head down and sighed. There was something else bothering her and she felt conflicted. She didn't want Faith to do the sex scenes, but if she tells her she can't, Faith will lose the movie. Consequences...actions and consequences.

Reece usually never thought about consequences for her actions. Now, Faith was suffering and it was all her fault. Could she really lose Faith for what she did tonight? All the small hairs on her body stood up in fear. Would flowers really work? Did she even have to know? Would Cori and Violet tell her? What would Faith do? Reece Corbett, whose mere presence caused grown men to piss their pants, suddenly found herself very scared of a little blond woman from Long Island.

†

After tossing and turning for what felt like hours, Faith eventually settled down in the guest bed with Cori and fell to sleep. It wasn't Reece, but it was a warm body and Faith needed to feel that presence.

When Reece came home, flowers in hand, nervous and sweating, the last thing she expected was a dark and quiet house. Relieved that there was no firing squad, she was still very weary of what lay in the dark.

"Faith?"

With no answer, she trudged upstairs to the bedroom, fully expecting an angry woman staring at her when she appeared. Finding the bed empty frightened her and she sat down to think, when she noticed Faith's clothes on the floor. Puzzled, she looked in the bathroom, and then even peered into the closet. "What the fuck?"

Returning downstairs, flipping on every light in the process, her nervousness reached a higher level. Not even Smudge came to greet her and she feared Faith had taken the dog and left. Sitting down dejectedly on the couch, she noticed two glasses on the coffee table and inspected them. Purple lipstick, she should have known. Cori had been here and she'd told Faith everything.

Reece panicked again, projecting her behavior onto her wife. Her thoughts took her to a bad place, a place where Faith was gallivanting with half naked women out of spite. Her head was swimming with stomach cramp inducing images.

The loud familiar snort emanating from the guest room was the sweetest sound she'd ever heard. Bolting up and into the room, she was surprised to see two bodies occupying the bed. Confused, she turned on the light and was instantly relieved to find Cori spooning her wife, and Smudge on Cori's head. She quickly retrieved the flowers from the living room and sat down next to Faith.

Faith drifted up from sleep in confusion. She was a little bit drunk and very groggy. She could swear Cori was caressing her and she couldn't understand. Making sense of the situation, she was coherent enough to realize that if Cori was touching her, she'd have to be on both sides of her and that made her open her eyes quickly. Startled by the strange object in her face, she jumped up.

Reece moved the flowers away and smiled weakly.

After gathering enough moisture in her mouth to speak, Faith cocked her head. "Reece? What is this?"

"Flowers."

Faith yawned loudly. "I can see that, but why?" She squinted at the clock. "Why now?"

Reece shrugged.

"Are you apologizing to me?"

"Yeah. Here." She thrust the flowers to Faith's chest.

"Baby, it's nearly four in the morning. Where the hell did you get flowers?"

"Never mind. Don't you like them?"

"Reece, I don't even know my name right now. How about we go to sleep and talk about this later."

Reece was disappointed. "But I want to listen to you. I'm supposed to listen to you."

Faith sighed and got out of bed. Of all the times Reece could have picked to act like this, now wasn't very good. "Okay. I just need water. Lots of water."

Triumphant, Reece marched out of the room to get water. Faith, still holding the flowers, met her halfway and they settled in the living room. The actress took the offered water and drank deeply.

"Faith, look...I'm an asshole."

Faith raised an eyebrow and waited.

"See, I'm proud of you and I don't tell you enough and I don't listen and I just yelled cuz I was mad and—"

Faith put up a finger, silently asking Reece to stop. "You are an asshole, and yes, you did yell like a maniac, but I expected that. You're right, you didn't listen, and that pissed me the hell off. I am having just as much trouble with this as you are, but you didn't give me the opportunity to tell you that. I don't want to do this movie."

Reece furrowed her brows. "But you're a great actress! You should do the movie, regardless of me."

"Not if it makes me uncomfortable. And, if it came down to doing the movie and losing you, the movie could rot. *But*, that would be my choice, not because you told me not to. Understand?"

Reece nodded and picked at a flower.

"Baby, I love you, and I don't want to make you sick. I don't want to make your stomach hurt and I certainly don't ever want you so mad at me again that you stomp off and act like an asshole."

Reece lowered her head. "I didn't do anything, I didn't even touch them," she mumbled.

Faith's eyes widened. "Who didn't you touch?"

"I thought Cori...but you said I was an asshole so I thought you knew—"

Faith's eyes narrowed. "What did you do?"

"Nothing! I didn't like it either!"

"Reece Corbett, did you act stupid with the dancers?"

"No!"

Faith fumed. "Reece!"

"Okay, a little stupid but I hated it and I stopped."

Faith shook her head. "Why do you do things like that? Who are you teaching a lesson to?"

Reece felt awful. "I don't know. I was mad."

"You were mad so you make a fool of me in the club?"

Reece made a face. "I didn't mean to do that. I was just...I don't know." She pushed the flowers closer to Faith. "I'm sorry?" she added, super quietly.

Faith craned her neck. "What?"

"I said, I'm sorry."

"You better be. What you did was uncalled for. There was no reason for you to run out of here and act like an ass. Not about this. Ooh! You make me so mad sometimes!"

Reece felt even more terrible. "I didn't think."

"No, you don't think. Reece, you have to stop running off in the moment because you're mad and deliberately trying to hurt who you're mad at!"

"Stop yelling at me, I feel bad enough."

Faith sighed. "What am I going to do with you?"

Reece shrugged. "You forgive me, right?"

"I'm mad at you, but I forgive you."

Reece grinned to herself. Faith wasn't going to leave her and she forgave her.

Faith drank the rest of the water. "I don't even want to do the sex scenes anyway. Your spiteful performance was pointless."

Reece looked up through her lashes. "What are you going to do?"

"I'm going to speak to the powers that be in a few hours and see if I can't change it."

"They better change it," Reece said angrily.

"Baby, if they don't, I don't do the movie. I'll be disappointed but I have principles, and a wife who I care about and don't want to hurt."

Reece felt better after hearing that and puffed up. "Want me to go with you and scare them?"

Faith chuckled. "No, honey, I think you need to stay far away from them." She took her wife's hand and held it.

Reece scooted closer to Faith. "Wanna do something dirty?"

"Now?" Faith asked in disbelief.

Reece leaned and peeked down the front of Faith's top. "Yeah, now."

The actress slapped her hand playfully. "I'm still mad at you."

"I can fix that." Reece boasted and lifted Faith, carrying her upstairs.

Chapter Seven

Cori awoke alone in the guest room and frowned. Figuring Faith got up early and didn't wake her, she got right out of bed. "Hon?" She peeked around the living room and kitchen and something caught her eye. "Flowers? Geez, these are lame." She picked them up and attempted to save their lives by putting them in a vase.

Assuming Reece got in late last night, she wasn't going to disturb her sleeping friends. Even though she was curious as hell to know what went on. The flowers were a good indication of Reece's attempt at an apology. Knowing Faith was bound to forgive her, she shook her head and chuckled. Faith was livid the night before. She was sure that Reece presenting flowers in the middle of the night made all the difference in the world.

†

Reece woke up before Faith and snuck out of bed with a gentle kiss to her wife. After a trip to the bathroom, she trudged down to the kitchen, exhausted but determined to make up for her bad behavior. Searching the fridge for breakfast, she yawned loudly and scratched her ass.

"That's attractive," Cori stated, reaching around Reece to get the coffee.

"Bite me," Reece muttered in a rather bored tone.

"Oooo, that's not the usual acid laced retort I'm accustomed to."

"I'm fucking tired, Cor. I hardly slept last night."

"That's because you were riddled with guilt."

"No, smart ass, that's because I was making up to my wife. Speaking of wife, why aren't you home?"

"For your information, while Faith was miserable and worried sick about you last night, I was here to console her. Her supportive wife seemed to be elsewhere, engaged in else-what."

"Fuck off, freak. Where the hell is the butter?"

Cori took the eggs from Reece and reached into the fridge for the butter. "Here, you big baby. What are we having?"

Reece dug around in the freezer for a box of Eggo's. "Faith and I are having eggs, waffles, and bacon. You are having a good trip on the subway home."

Cori started scrambling eggs. "You think a breakfast will clear you of any wrongdoings?"

"For your information, Faith already forgave me. Besides, we have a bigger problem than my behavior. Faith is all fucked up about this script. She's going to call the guy in charge this morning and try and get him to change it."

Cori narrowed her eyes. "Yeah, I know and he better change it, or else."

"What if he doesn't?" Reece asked nervously. "If he doesn't, then Faith won't do the movie and she'll be miserable."

"You ain't kidding. Let's not think about the worst. He wrote it for her, let's just wait and see."

†

Faith awoke to the smell of bacon wafting through her senses. By the time she got to the kitchen, Reece already had breakfast on the table. "What's all this about?"

Reece grinned. "It's for you. I made it," she said proudly.

The actress kissed her wife on the cheek and sat down. "Ooo, a slice of orange and everything."

"That was my idea," Cori called from the living room.

"Are you still here?" Reece asked, pouring coffee.

Cori ignored her friend and kissed Faith on the head. "I'm going. I just wanted to see you this morning. Is everything okay?"

"Yeah, I suppose." Faith looked to Reece who smiled. "I forgive her, but I'm still a little mad."

Cori stuck her tongue out at Reece. "Call me if you need anything, hon."

Reece waited until Cori left. "Are you really still mad at me?"

"Yes."

"But I thought we made up?"

"We made love, not made up. Anyway, I don't hate you, baby, I'm just mad at what you did. You didn't think about anyone but yourself when you went off and acted like a moron."

Reece sighed. "Can I do anything?"

"Breakfast is a good start. These eggs are great! What did you do?"

"I made them with love."

Faith rolled her eyes. "Oh, man, you really are trying."

Reece showed all her teeth in a smile.

Faith swallowed and sighed. "I have to call Brad."

"Brad? Why him? I thought you were going to call whoever wrote the script." Reece's eyebrows knit together.

Faith speared some waffle. "Brad's my agent, he should do the dirty work, don't you think? Besides, if I get on the phone with the writer I'll go off and that's not a good thing."

Reece pursed her lips. "Yeah, I guess you're right."

Faith sat in thought for a little while before speaking again. "Reece, are you going to be all right with *any* body contact between me and another woman?"

Reece grumbled.

"The truth, please."

"Faith, I don't know. Would you if it were me?"

The actress contemplated that. "No. I wouldn't be okay, but I guess I'd have to accept it."

Reece got annoyed. "Oh, so you mean I have to accept it, too? What if I hate it?"

"It's part of my job, baby. Just one small part of it. You're smart enough to know it's not real."

"I know that," Reece replied defensively. "I just don't like it."

"But there's going to be some contact, Reece. It's not like I'm emotionally attached to her or anything. It's just acting."

"Who's her anyway?"

Faith squirmed uncomfortably. "The rumor mill says Alicia Alvarez"

Reece exploded out of her chair. "*Alicia Alvarez*? No way! No fucking way!"

"Baby! I didn't pick her!"

Reece fumed as she stomped around the kitchen. "Not that bitch. There is no way!"

"Reece! It's just acting!" Faith tried to calm her extremely irate wife.

"My *ass*! You want that woman! You *told* me you do! And now you'll be kissing her? That's cheating!" Reece banged on the counter with both hands.

"No it's not. It's acting," Faith said quietly, not quite believing it herself.

"Your lips are not touching that woman!" Reece banged out of the room.

"Reece! Don't do this."

"Leave me alone, Faith." Reece had her keys in her hand. She was really angry. "I need to go out."

Faith listened to the door slam and shrunk down in her chair. "That went well."

†

Reece thought she was angry before, but now, she was furious. She kicked a garbage pail and raged. "Alicia Alvarez! Of all the fucking women in this world…*her*?"

She walked aimlessly, knowing that, for some reason, getting out of the house was the right thing to do. She wanted to scream at Faith, tell her *no* and insist she forget the movie. Somewhere inside she knew that wasn't the right thing to do, so she ran away. "How can I deal with this? How does she expect me to deal with this? I can't! I'll throw up if I have to hear about it. Oh God, I'll have to go to this movie when it opens!"

†

Cori left the bagel store to find Reece leaning on a car, arms folded tightly, jaw clenching. She hadn't been gone fifteen minutes! What the hell happened? She approached her carefully. "Reece?"

Reece lifted her angry gaze from her feet to the dancer. "Leave me alone."

Cori got slightly closer. "What happened?"

Reece pushed off the car, arms flying, face twisted. "Alicia Alvarez? Did you fucking know that?"

Cori swallowed hard. "Uh...yeah."

Reece kicked a tree. "Great! This is fucking great!"

"Reece, people are starting to stare. Come on, let's walk."

"I don't want to walk. I want to kill something!"

Cori smirked at a curious passerby. "You heard her. She wants to kill something so I'd get moving." She turned to Reece again who looked about to blow her top. "Reece, c'mon, let's go home."

"*Home*! No way. I can't look at Faith right now. I just keep seeing her fucking that tramp. I can't."

"Reece! It's not real, you ass! Stop behaving like an idiot! My toasted bagel is getting soggy."

"Fuck your bagel, Cori, and fuck you. You don't understand."

"Fine, be a moron. I'm going home. I suggest you get over it real soon."

Cori walked away and Reece flung herself against the tree she'd kicked earlier. "Stupid freak doesn't get it. Fucking Alicia."

†

Violet listened to Cori's rehash of what happened and sighed. "Man, oh, man. Alicia Alvarez. She's like a walking condom, she has so many different men. I can imagine Reece's anger."

"Anger ain't the word, Vi. She's inconsolable. Anyway, maybe it's a good idea she gets lost in this mood. Faith has enough stress and doesn't need Reece's immaturity." Cori sat in her lover's lap. "What did you say to her last night? She came home with flowers."

Violet chuckled then kissed Cori's nose. "Nothing deep. Looks like she may be home with more flowers later though."

"Who knows? She's real pissed. She seemed to be coping with the whole sex thing until Alicia came up."

Violet thought for a moment. "She may be hot, but she's a ho. Maybe if we convince Faith that Alicia Alvarez is nothing but a sperm burping gutter slut, she'll lose her crush."

"Ew, pretty attractive description. Good luck convincing Faith though."

†

Unable to finish breakfast, Faith sat on the couch, arms folded. Reece's behavior was getting tiresome and she wished her wife would just get past it all. She reached down to Smudge, who was watching her curiously. Picking him up and placing him on her lap, she sighed. "You understand me. You get that it's just a movie."

Smudge licked her nose with his tiny pink tongue.

"See, you love me. You don't care if it's Alicia Alvarez or not."

Smudge cocked his little head to the side in a question. Faith felt she needed to reply. "What?" The dog sat down and stared at Faith. She swore it was in an accusatory manner. "Oh, I see. You, too. Fine." Faith stuck out her chin in defiance.

Smudge stood up and yapped.

Faith leaned her head back on the couch in defeat. "I know, I know, you're right. She has every right to be jealous. I know if it were her and Angelina Jolie, I'd bust a vessel. What do I do? Even if I get them to take out the hardcore stuff, I'll still have to make out with the woman." Faith thought about that for a while, and realized it did give her a little thrill.

Stop thinking like that, this is strictly business. You can't enjoy it, that'd be cheating.

She sat up and picked up the script from the coffee table. Leafing through it, she stopped on one particularly graphic scene. "Oh yeah, Reece can't handle this. I can't handle this so how can I expect her to. Smudge, I'm so fucked. I gotta call Brad."

†

Reece wandered around aimlessly for a while before reluctantly returning home. She opened the door quietly and slipped in heading straight for Smudge. Scooping him off Faith's lap, and gathering his ear medicine from the coffee table, she brought him up to the bedroom, ignoring her wife. As soon as she settled down on the bed, she heard Faith approaching the door.

"I didn't think you'd be back so soon."

Reece didn't look up. "Believe me, I didn't want to, but he needs his medicine."

Faith sat on the bed. "You can't stay mad at me. Reece, you have to understand. Please."

"All I know is you wanted to do Alicia since the first time you saw her and now you'll be rolling around like naked pigs for everyone to see. I understand you'll be liking it a lot. That's all I need to understand."

Faith watched as Reece pulled a small bit of cotton from a cotton ball, wet it with solution, and gently wiped out the dog's ear. She smiled despite the situation. *Reece has it in her. She has the ability to be gentle, when it counts.*

"There you go, little man. Shake it out."

Smudge shook his head so hard he fell down.

Reece picked him up. "Just a little drop or two of antibiotic and we're done." She held his head in her hand, the hand swallowing the tiny dog's whole face.

Faith watched the scene with envy. "You're so gentle with him. Why are you so aggressive with me?"

"He's not cheating on me."

Faith threw her hands up. "Reece, if it were anyone else, would you be acting this way?"

Reece shrugged. She really didn't know.

"You were okay with me kissing Jim on television."

"That was Jim the dim. Besides, I had a talk with him." Reece smiled to herself. "Maybe I should have a talk with Alicia."

"No way!" Faith protested. "I will not have you threatening that poor woman."

Reece cut her off, angry again. "Since when is she that poor woman? Because you want her?"

Faith sat closer to her wife and touched her face. "Just calm down, already. We have to solve this, Reece. I don't want it tearing us apart."

Reece steeled her jaw and said nothing.

"Baby, please. I love you. This has to work out. You have to deal with it. Please. I know you're the strongest woman I ever met, you can do this," Faith pleaded.

Reece sighed and lifted her gaze for the first time to meet Faith's. "I'm trying, Faith. I'm trying. I'm selfish and I don't share well. I don't think I can stomach this."

The last sentence was so quiet Faith had to strain to hear it. She wrapped her arms around Reece and sighed. "Just hold me, baby. I need you to hold me so I know it's all right."

Reece wrapped her arms around her wife and closed her eyes. She had to let Faith do her thing. She knew she had to but it was going to hurt. Badly.

"I love you, Reece."

"Me too."

Despite their love, the tension was a bit thick in the Corbett-Ashford household. Faith eventually and reluctantly left Reece up in the bedroom with Smudge while she went downstairs to resume her phone calls. She left another message with her agent, Brad, and made a call to Mr. Wells, the gentleman that assured her of the part when she went to audition. Without anyone else to call, she waited impatiently for a response.

†

Reece made her way downstairs after a long while and announced that she was going to the gym.

Faith watched her put on her sneakers. "Don't be so angry, Reece, please."

"I'm fine," she replied flatly.

"Oh, that was convincing," Faith replied sarcastically.

Reece turned to Faith and sighed. "Look, I'm not okay with this and before I act like an ass again, I'm going to the gym. I think I learned my lesson and the weights don't talk back. Just let me leave without annoying me about it."

Faith's eyebrow raised high. Reece just spoke more words to her in that instant than she had for days. "Okay, you go, but don't hurt yourself. You're not Hercules."

Reece nodded as she left.

Faith stared at the door silently.

†

Reece walked sullenly to the gym, a lot on her mind. She was conflicted.

Faith has a job, not just a job, but her dream job. She wanted this more than anything. Moving to New York City all alone, with nothing, leaving her parents against their wishes, working shit jobs, living in a slum. All in the name of an acting career.

Reece sighed loudly, knowing full well what her own job asked of her and asked of Faith. She felt guilty for her negative feelings. Surrounded by naked women all night, having to audition new ones, watch the acts of regulars to gauge the response levels. She knew in her heart she would never want Faith to do what she did, yet Faith never complained. Could Faith be more trusting than she was? Reece sulked.

But I don't want her kissing Alicia Alvarez. She's my wife, and I have a say don't I? Why does this even have to happen anyway? Sure, I want her to be in a movie, that's what she wants, that makes her happy.

Reece scowled hard. She knew she really didn't have a say one way or another. The only way to stop it was to put the fear of God in Alicia and Faith was on to that plan. Not wanting to think about it anymore, Reece opened the door to the gym. The smell of sweat, the blast of manufactured cold air greeted her like an old friend. Feeling immediately more comfortable, she strode to the locker room with long steps.

†

Faith busied herself cleaning the house while she waited for someone to call her back. Then it happened. While she was on her knees, cleaning under the couch, the phone rang. Rushing to get it, she smacked her head on the coffee table and cursed all the way to the phone. Filled with anxiety she grabbed the phone. "Hello?"

"Hello, this is the vet's office. We'd like to know how Goliath is feeling."

"Goliath?" Faith questioned.

"Goliath Corbett? Did I call the wrong number?"

Faith rolled her eyes. "No, you have the right number. He's doing pretty well, I think. My wife is actually taking care of his ear."

"Ah, yes, Ms. Corbett. We're quite familiar with her."

Faith felt bad for the poor woman. "I'll have her call you as soon as she gets home. But I can tell you she is taking very good care of Goliath."

"Good to know. If anything changes, feel free to call."

After the phone call ended, Faith sat down next to Smudge on the floor. "So, why didn't you tell me about the new name? Do you think it suits you, sweetie?" She kissed the tiny dog on the nose and laughed lightly. "Goliath, huh?" Faith held the little dog in one hand up to her face. Smudge licked her lips. "Oh yes, totally suitable, you big killer dog."

†

Reece worked hard to forget her troubles. She focused all of her concentration on the particular muscle she was working. Her already taxed biceps bulged as she curled the barbell. She was squeezing her triceps on the extension and then squeezing her bicep as she curled the heavy weight. She concentrated on the feeling of her muscles working, pleasurable pain as she exhausted her negative energy. Unable to do one more curl, she dropped the heavy iron with a loud bang and stretched her arms. Women and men alike watched her, watched her muscles flex and bulge, watched the sweat drip down her neck into her cleavage, and watched her ass as she twisted this way and that. Reece knew they were finding sensuality where she found her only innocent escape.

No doubt about it, Reece was worth a second look, by any breathing human, but she was oblivious to it. No game playing today, no toying with the straight men, only release from her worries. It was extremely cathartic. Before her religious attachment to the gym, Reece had been violent, aggressive, and unmanageable when angry. Little by little, she learned that the gym might be her only relief from herself. And she benefited greatly for her efforts. Finished stretching and ready for the shower, Reece took a moment to catch her breath. Looking around at her various admirers, she smirked; glad she wasn't aware of it all before.

†

Antsy and irritated, Faith began going through the script and changing the questionable scenes herself. She began to distance herself from the part and started picturing the scenes as she created the changes. When she was sufficiently satisfied with the editing, she put the script down and felt a sense of satisfaction. While in the moment, she called Brad, her agent and was surprised when he picked up the phone.

"Brad, I couldn't wait for all the red tape and changed the script myself. I think it's doable and want to know how to get it to the right people. "

Brad was surprised. "You changed it yourself? You're a writer now?"

"Maybe, and I'm pretty proud of what I did."

Brad made a small sound. "I'll get it to the right people, but I can't guarantee this will fly."

"Whatever you have to do, Brad. You just make sure to tell them that your high profile lesbian client won't do it any other way," Faith said smugly.

Brad chuckled. "Okay. I'll do it. I'll send someone to pick it up."

Faith hung up the phone, feeling infinitely better. She wished Reece were there so she could share her news.

†

Reece, rejuvenated, had a bounce in her step as she headed home. Not thinking at all refreshed her, and the endorphins she was currently experiencing made her almost happy. Almost. Still there in the back of her mind, like a little knot of tension that you can't get to, remained. It didn't matter, though. Reece continued her trek home, keeping the knot behind the bone so she didn't have to touch it. She veered into a bakery, and bought Faith's favorite pastry as if on autopilot.

†

Faith was happy to hear Reece's key in the door. She wasn't expecting her wife to come home until much later. Now, she just had to wonder what mood Reece was in after such a short time away. Eyeing the striped bag in Reece's hand, Faith smiled.

"You just bring that little bag in here," she instructed.

Reece grinned and obeyed, surprising Faith with a short kiss.

"Wow. It must have been a great work out!"

Reece nodded. "It was."

Faith inhaled deeply. "Ooo, get back here, you smell so good."

Reece chuckled under her breath. "I took a shower there." She sat down on the couch next to her wife, and it felt good to feel Faith's breath on her neck. "You better eat that thing and leave my neck alone. There are too many endorphins flying around in my blood."

"And that's a bad thing?" Faith took a bite of the pastry. "Mmm."

"Well, it is if you're still mad at me."

"Reece, I can be mad at you and still love you and make love with you."

Reece grinned widely. "Yeah? You wanna?"

Faith smacked her wife playfully. "Not this second. I have to tell you something."

"Okay, what? Did the guy call you back?"

"No, but I took matters into my own hands and changed the script myself. Brad sent someone to pick it up. Now, all we do is wait."

Reece raised her eyebrows. "You can do that?"

"I don't know. Brad isn't sure they'll take it seriously. It's a gamble. They say they wrote it for me, so if they mean that, they'll fix it. If not, they can get someone else to play the part."

"For real? You would want that?" Reece leaned forward and took a bite of Faith's pastry.

"No, not really. I want this part, but not if it means porn. I'm going to make sure there's a no nudity clause in the rest of my contracts from now on."

Reece smiled with relief. "Now, that's more like it. Hurry up and eat that so I can get you naked and lick your whole body."

Chapter Eight

As Faith was swallowing the last bit of pastry, Reece began to undress. She peeled off her tank top, exposing her full breasts and threw the shirt on the floor. She reached eagerly for Faith, but the actress backed away and stood up.

"No, watch me." Faith started to move to an imaginary beat, swaying and dancing as she slowly slid her pants down, revealing a barely there thong. She spun around slowly, giving her wife a full view of her ass cheeks as she stepped out of the pants.

Reece grinned and leaned back on the couch, enjoying the show.

Faith lifted her shirt slowly, partially exposing her breasts, swaying her hips seductively at Reece. Wiggling her ass, and swaying, she shimmied all the way to the floor and back up again. She could feel Reece's pleasure rising from where she stood.

Reece stared wolfishly at Faith's ass. No matter how many naked girls she watched dance at work, no one could do to her what Faith did. She swallowed hard as the object of her desire turned around topless.

Faith danced, sliding her hands up from her waist to cup her breasts and she tweaked her nipples for both their benefits.

Reece's eyes narrowed and her nipples hardened in empathy. "Oh, yeah, baby, you dance for me."

Faith leaned forward and licked her lips, humming as she did. "You wanna touch them?" she asked in a sexy voice.

"What do you think?" Reece replied, already reaching out.

Faith danced away from her reach. "How about we let them touch you?" she teased, climbing on to the couch, on her knees, next to Reece. She leaned into her wife and dragged her breasts along Reece's arm. The contact made her shiver and her nipples got even stiffer. "Mmm."

Reece closed her eyes and concentrated on the feel of the pert nipples sliding up and down her arm. Suddenly, Faith straddled her lap and leaned in. Their nipples touched and Reece was the one to shiver. "Yeah, you're just a horny little thing, aren't you?"

Faith hummed. "I have the greatest incentive." She got to her knees and brought her breasts to Reece's face and began to tease her with them.

Reece attempted to grab one in her mouth but Faith was too quick. Reece went to grab them with her hands and Faith stopped her.

Faith held both her lover's hands and shook her head. "No touching." Reece's eyebrows leapt up. "Humor me. Just for a little while."

Reece cracked a grin. "A little while, but what I catch is mine."

"Fair's fair," Faith replied, dragging her breasts across Reece's face. She tried to avoid her wife's open mouth as best she could, but Reece was ready and sucked the pierced nipple into her mouth. Faith first grunted in surprise but the sound became a purr of arousal. "Ooo, you're quick, baby," she said, pressing herself against her wife.

Reece nodded, too involved in her treat to respond out loud. She wanted to switch to the other nipple but when she let go, Faith backed away.

"Remember, you're humoring me."

Reece sighed and licked her lips. "For a little while only," she agreed with a grin.

Faith let go of Reece's hands and ran her own along Reece's well-defined arms, savoring each muscle. "You're almost too good." She ran her fingers up and across Reece's shoulders, dug her nails in and smooshed her breasts in her wife's face. "I love these shoulders, they're so perfect."

Reece's arousal cranked up a few notches. She liked it when Faith was naughty. "What else do you love?" she asked, purposely flexing her abs, hoping for an inspection.

Faith caught on and leered at Reece's stomach. "I love that stomach." She slid slowly down Reece's legs and kissed her tight stomach in four places. "I bet it tastes as good as it smells." She poked her tongue out and tasted with a long, soft swipe, leaving a damp trail. "Oh, yeah, delicious."

Reece shivered as Faith blew on her stomach. Reaching down, she pulled Faith up to face her, covering her mouth with her own. Their tongues met immediately, tangling and dueling. Reece groaned as Faith sucked her tongue, feeling the pull between her legs. She broke away from the kiss, slightly breathless and very turned on. "Okay, you can finish now." She pushed Faith back down. "I just needed a kiss."

"I'm not complaining. Where was I?"

Reece pointed downwards. "Tasting my abs, if I recall."

"Oh, yeah." Faith licked across Reece's hard belly with a flat tongue. "Baby, baby, baby, I love it when your muscles move under my tongue." She licked in the opposite direction, and Reece twitched again, just how Faith liked it. "I can smell you already," she whispered, bringing her face to Reece's crotch and inhaling.

"Uh huh," Reece agreed, unable to speak real words as Faith kissed her hot crotch.

"You want it bad, don't you," Faith stated, glancing up at Reece to find her watching. "Lift up and I'll take off these shorts."

Reece lifted up her ass and Faith practically tore off the shorts and underwear in one tug, tossing them over her shoulder. "You can't believe how much I want this," Faith murmured as she bent her head.

Reece groaned as Faith made a tiny swipe with her tongue.

"I think I'll tease this pussy for a while. What do you think?"

Reece narrowed her eyes and threaded her fingers through her wife's hair. "I don't think so."

The actress grinned devilishly. "I do, and you're gonna take it because you love me." She ran her tongue lightly up the length of Reece's sex, backing up as Reece tried to move closer. "No, no, just relax," Faith whispered.

"You're in for it, you know that." Reece groaned, her head falling heavily against the back of the couch.

"I'm counting on it."

Reece managed half a chuckle at Faith's remark before she moaned deeply. Her wife suddenly licked her hard, lingering for a moment on her clit. "Oh yeah…"

"Mmm hmm. I know you like it, baby." Faith was feeling mighty cocky that Reece was allowing her free rein and she took full advantage of it. She wrapped her arms under and around her thighs and tried to hold her in place. Reece was much stronger than she was and was trying hard to get what she wanted.

"Stay there, baby," Reece urged.

Faith lingered at Reece's hard clit for a few seconds, drawing a pleasured groan from her lover. Slowly she brought her tongue lower and teased the waiting entrance. She circled the opening slowly and barely used any pressure.

Reece squirmed from the tickling sensation and began to give Faith a mental countdown until she took what she wanted. She gritted her teeth and flared her nostrils against the sensual attack, breathing heavily and erratically.

Faith drew her tongue up, around, across, down, and even poked the tip inside, teasing her lover mercilessly. She relished in the taste and textures her tongue met with each swipe. She hummed her delight as she tasted and licked, reveling in the sensation of Reece's hard thighs flexing and straining.

Reece groaned, and bucked in pleasure as Faith drew her clit in between her puckered lips. Without warning, she clamped her strong thighs around her wife's head and grabbed her hair with both large hands. "Enough humoring, make me come."

Faith gasped at the sudden display of strength and immediately obeyed. She was satisfied enough at Reece's patience so far and was more than happy to make her come. She concentrated on the swollen clit in her mouth and sucked it hard.

Reece blew out a loud breath of relief and ecstasy, her thighs trembling in anticipation of release. Her muscles clenched and spasmed as she began to come.

Faith whimpered her own pleasure as her lover's orgasm took control. She pictured that gorgeous face in blissful release, her own clit throbbing in empathy.

Reece opened her thighs and let go of Faith's head, pulling her up quickly and pushing her down onto her back. "My turn now," she said, breathless and intent. She climbed to her knees at Faith's feet, grabbed both ankles, and threw the smaller woman's legs over her shoulders. "You're so fucking wet for me." She grabbed Faith's ass cheeks in her hands and raised her even higher.

"Reece!" Faith gasped as she practically dangled from her lover's shoulders. "God!"

Reece wasted no time burying her face entirely in Faith's sex, thrusting her tongue inside like a hot spear.

Faith tried to react, attempted to thrust her hips, but was helpless as she lay on only her shoulders and head. "Baby, yes!"

Reece grunted and growled as she lapped up as much sweet ambrosia as she could, fucking her lover with her tongue, shaking her head back and forth to drive Faith crazy.

Faith moaned a high pitched sound as Reece's nose drove back and forth against her hard clit, her thick tongue plunging in and out, driving her quickly to the edge of oblivion. "Oh, God, Reece, it's coming already—"

Reece snaked an arm out from under Faith and plunged two fingers inside to replace her tongue which she was now using as a weapon across Faith's throbbing clit. "Mmm, mmm," she hummed as Faith's inner walls began to clench on her fingers.

"Reece! Baby!"

Reece opened her eyes and looked down the length of Faith's body. Her breasts were heaving, her face red, her lips full and wet as gasps of pleasure escaped them. She twitched and writhed, her sex grabbing at Reece's fingers like a vise as she came. Reece drew out the orgasm, watching through hungry eyes as Faith thrashed and groaned. Then slowly, she removed her fingers and eased up on her oral assault, leaving tiny kisses on Faith's pulsating sex. "You have the hottest pussy," she whispered, carefully lowering her wife from the awkward position.

Faith, panting, wrapped her legs around her lover's waist and opened her arms. "C'mere, baby."

Reece pulled Faith up gently by her arms until she was sitting on her lap and wrapped her strong arms around her. "You taste so good."

Faith sighed in Reece's embrace. "You feel so good. "

They sat like that for a long while, wrapped in one another's arms, until Reece stretched out on the couch. Faith crawled on top of her, and they both drifted off into a well-deserved nap.

†

Faith wandered around the house aimlessly after Reece left for work. No one returned any of her calls, not even Brad. She tried watching TV for a while but was bored to death with it. She looked out of the window, watched the people go by, and had a sudden urge to do the same. Calling for

Smudge, she hooked his leash on and went for a walk, knowing Reece would never want her out by herself at night.

It was a nice evening, the breeze was blowing, the air was clear and Faith calmed quickly. Smudge sniffed and poked at everything he could and Faith enjoyed a rare opportunity to walk him. Reece, despite what she would admit, was the real mommy. She walked him, fed him, inspected, and picked at him constantly. Faith smiled to herself when she recalled the day Reece thought Smudge had the flu because he sneezed. The dog sniffed at dust under the bed and sneezed three times in a row. Reece panicked, immediately assuming he was dying, blaming Cori for giving the dog her cold. Truth was Cori had allergies, and dogs can't catch human colds, but Reece wasn't hearing it. Faith warmed up inside while thinking about how gentle and soft her big bad wife behaved with the dog. *Goliath*, she thought with a laugh. Just as she finished giggling, her cell phone rang. It was Reece. *Shit, she's going to kill me.* "Hi, baby,"

"Where are you?"

"In front of the house," Faith lied.

"Why? Didn't I tell you it's not safe for you at night, after that last crazy?"

Faith frowned. "I'm fine, Reece. Besides, I have Goliath to protect me."

Reece remained silent.

"I know all about it so you don't even have to try and explain." Faith said, smiling.

Reece cleared her throat. "It's just that Smudge is such...you know and me being so...and Goliath just sounds better."

Faith grinned. "I thought so. Now go back to work and let me enjoy the night."

"I just wanted to know if you heard from anyone yet."

"No, no one. That's why I needed to get out of the house. I'm obsessing about the phone. Baby, I'm fine by myself."

Reece scowled. "I don't like it, but I'm not there so I can't pick you up and carry you inside."

"Reece, I'm fine. There are no crazies out here. I swear."

"Fine."

Faith pictured her wife's steely-jawed look. "I love you."

"Yeah, me too."

Faith smiled at the phone after her overprotective lover hung up. "She's just being herself, Smudge. Anyway, we better start home, someone may have called."

As she turned to walk away, she realized there were three young women following her. She sighed at their loud whispers arguing whether or not she was 'the actress'. She wondered if she should turn around and announce herself but decided to keep walking. Soon enough, there they were standing beside her.

"Faith Ashford! Oh, my God! I knew it was you! Can you sign this for me?"

"Where's your hunky wife?

"You're shorter in person."

"Man, you're hot!"

Faith closed her eyes and sighed again, then turned around. "I don't have a pen, ladies, I'm sorry."

"Oh, I have one! Can you sign my bra?"

Faith's eyes widened. "Uh, my wife would kill me if I signed your bra. How about a piece of paper?"

The young lady rooted through her backpack until she came up with paper.

After Faith signed all the papers, and one shoe, she hurried home. It's not that she didn't feel grateful for admirers—but some were overzealous. Like the crazy Reece was talking about who had grabbed her and kissed her on the mouth. Reece flipped out and nearly killed the young dyke, and to tell the truth, Faith was pretty shaken up too.

Closing the door behind her, she relaxed into her safe house.

†

Reece took her usual seat at the bar and surveyed her club. It was crowded. It was always crowded. She watched the bargirls serve while smiling, winking, and flirting. Their tip jars were always full. Nodding to herself in satisfaction, she looked toward the main stage while Cori did her "jungle girl" routine. Men of all ages and sizes offered money to the dancer, hoping she'd come to them with her attention. Cori had been dancing at the club for a long time now and had made a pretty big name for herself. Rival clubs routinely sent spies in to watch Reece's girls, studying them, wanting to be them. As a rule, women weren't allowed into gentleman's clubs, but Reece had a women's night, laughing in the face of the law, and it was her best night of the week. Now and again, she'd have some women's rights protesters form a little huddle on the sidewalk, but after a few weeks, the media attention would die down. Thanks to that media attention though, her club was famous, and on weekends, it wasn't unusual to find a line waiting to get in. The titty club owned by a lesbian, married to an actress who used to work there. It was all pretty scandalous.

Reece watched Cori maneuver around the stage expertly in her stilettos despite the flashing lights and nodded again to herself. Cori was important to Reece, not only as a star dancer, but also as a friend. She smiled at the dancer. Cori knew how much Reece depended on her and Reece knew she didn't have to voice it. Which was good, because Reece didn't voice much.

Cori caught Reece's eye and winked, then bent and flashed her ass. Reece chuckled and swiveled her stool to look toward the door. Sarge, the bouncer, was studying somebody's ID intently.

Reece pursed her lips in thought, wondering how she ever got so lucky to have so many loyal employees. They didn't have to stay when she inherited the club. They loved Frankie so much that Reece was surprised they didn't hate her for taking his place. Sarge eventually turned the man away and Reece was comfortable that Sarge had her reasons. She trusted Sarge. She trusted Cori. It wasn't their club, but they protected it like it was. It left Reece a little room to breathe when she came to work at night. She was grateful. Maybe she'd have to let them know one day.

There was uproar and Reece didn't have to look to know Cori just became naked onstage. She didn't watch Cori when she was nude. It just didn't feel right to Reece. She wasn't sure why, but it didn't. The only time she came close was when Faith and Cori danced that night together. Reece's lips formed an evil grin as she recalled that night, and what happened afterwards. Thinking of Faith naked, suddenly brought thoughts of the movie. Unpleasant thoughts. Shaking them loose, Reece stood and disappeared to her office.

†

Faith peeled off her clothes and headed for the bathroom. She had already filled the tub, lit candles, put on music, and poured herself a glass of wine. She slid into the hot water with a loud sigh of pleasure. A while back, Reece came home with one of those inflatable neck pillows that stuck to the tub. At first Faith wasn't sure she'd ever use such a thing, but tonight she decided to try it out. Leaning back, the pillow fit right under her neck and she wondered how she ever took a bath without one.

Just as she was drifting off, she heard Reece come home. Confused, she sat up. "Baby?" she called out.

"Yeah."

"What are you doing home?" Faith was worried.

Reece entered the bathroom and smiled at her wife. "I was in my office, and well…" She sat at the edge of the tub. "I got to thinking."

"That could be dangerous," Faith teased.

Reece made a face. "No, really, I was thinking about the movie. I was thinking about how you trust me at my job, with naked girls and my reputation. I don't know, all that thinking was making me crazy and I realized I have to be okay with whatever you want to do. I trust you. I guess what I'm saying is for you do that movie and I'll be fine. I have to be."

Faith grinned from ear to ear. "I love you, Reece. Thank you." She held out her hand and Reece took it, grasping it firmly.

"I know you love me, and it makes all the difference in the world. I don't remember a time when I didn't love you. I need to stop behaving like you're my possession."

Faith smiled. "You were talking to Cori weren't you?"

Reece looked down. "A little."

"Well, good. You should listen to her more. Now, come here." Faith yanked Reece hard and she fell into the tub with a big splash.

"Faith! I can't believe you did that!" Reece righted herself as best she could and wiped the hair out of her face.

"You won't shrink. Just kiss me and stop complaining."

Chapter Nine

Cori pushed Violet down onto the bed and crawled between her open legs. "Spread 'em for me, woman, I'm hungry."

Violet threw her legs over her lover's shoulders and begged. "Please, baby, I'm so ready."

Just as Cori licked her lips, the phone began to ring. "You have got to be kidding me!"

Violet grabbed her girlfriend's bright pink hair and pulled her head down. "You'd better ignore it," she warned.

Cori stuck her tongue out and took a long lick. "Mmmm…"

Just then, Faith's voice screamed through the room. "I did it! I did it! They're using my changes!"

Cori sat up, excited about the news.

"Get back down there, Cori," Violet begged.

"Stop having sex and pick up the phone or I'm going to start singing."

Violet ran for the phone. "Hello! Please, don't start singing."

Faith laughed. "What took you so long?"

"We really were having sex, you know."

"I feel for you." Faith tittered.

Cori grabbed the phone away. "So they really are gonna use your changes? How fucking cool is that?"

"I know!" Faith gushed. "I feel so relieved, and proud!"

Violet leaned toward the phone. "What did Reece say?"

"She doesn't know, she's at the gym, I can't wait to tell her! She'll be so happy."

Cori frowned. "I dunno, Faith. You're still tits to the wind so I can't see her doing a happy dance."

"Look, she has to accept it. She may not like it at all, but at least she's going to try. Thanks for talking to her last night, by the way. You really helped."

Cori nodded in acknowledgement. "Yeah, well, it's the least I can do. She still has issues, no matter what she says to you."

"I know, but she's going to deal with it her own way. Soon enough she'll be better with it. We had a talk this morning and she said as long as I don't tell her what's going on, she'll deal better."

Cori snorted. "Oh, and it'll be better for it to slap her in the face during the premiere? I don't think so."

Faith paused. "Shit."

"Yeah, a big stinking shit."

†

Reece headed for the showers and was stopped in her tracks by the gym owner. Rolling her eyes, she put a hand on her hip and waited.

"Hi, we talked a while back, remember?"

Reece nodded and looked bored.

"You know, the offer still stands to work here. I've been watching you, as have a lot of other people and I'm sure you'd never want for clients."

Reece glanced around at the gym. Yes, there were numerous admirers, mostly women. Her eyes narrowed and she didn't know why. "Okay, talk to me," she said folding her arms. "What kind of deal can we make?"

†

Faith, the dog in her lap, clad in Reece's tank top from the night before, leaned back in the kitchen chair with her coffee. Smiling, she absently petted Smudge. She was feeling rather smug about getting her way. Nothing could change her mood.

Except what was waiting on the doorstep outside.

The actress frowned at the sound of the doorbell, and yelled her way toward the door. "Baby, you have to stop

123

forgetting your keys!" Opening the door, she stepped back in horror.

"Surprise!"

†

Reece shook hands with the gym owner and with a smug smile gathered her things and left, not even showering.

Not bad, she thought as she walked out. I pick up my own clients, it's my money. He gets me a client, he gets a cut. A small cut, and I get free use of the gym. Gotta wear the stupid shirt, but there could be worse things.

Reese felt a little pang of discomfort with what she just did, but blew it off. Faith's gonna be busy with the movie, and I'm not just gonna sit there and do nothing. I need a hobby, too. I can't tell the clients what to wear, I mean they have to wear very little so I can see the muscles at work. It's not like they're naked. She rationalized her actions. Barely.

†

Faith watched as her mother dragged in bags. She eyed the luggage with disdain. "Mom, how long *are* you here for?"

Marsha, Faith's mom, made a face. "No, hello? No hug?" She held out her arms and waited.

Faith walked into them and sighed. There was really nothing she could do. "Sorry. I'm happy you're here." *Yeah, right.*

"Now, that's better." Marsha walked into the living room on her way to the guest room and stopped at the coffee table. Reaching for the script, she lit up excitedly. "Oooo, what's this?"

Faith grabbed the script back. "Nothing, Mom, nothing. Go get settled."

Marsha gave her daughter a sideways glance. "All right," she said, looking over her shoulder at the script as she dragged her bag into the guest room.

Faith threw herself into the couch and mimed a fit.

When Reece walked in, she saw her wife lying on the couch, kicking and screaming silently, hugging the script. "And you're doing that because…"

Faith jumped up and settled herself. "Reece, we have to talk."

"Yeah, but me first," Reece said, standing in front of the couch.

"No, Reece—"

Reece silenced Faith with a finger. "I took that job at the gym," she declared.

Faith looked incredulous. "You what?"

"I took the trainer's job. I start tomorrow."

Faith gritted her teeth. "You spiteful little…*argh!* Reece, we can't talk about this now, but we will. Oh, we will."

"What's wrong with a hobby?"

"Hobby?" Faith's eyes almost turned red. In a hushed voice, she spoke through her teeth. "What were you thinking? We have a visitor right now, so you are really lucky. I could kill you."

"Visitor?" Reece looked toward the guest room. "Who the hell…."

"Theresa? Is that you?"

Reece paled. "Oh, no. No, no, no, no. Not your mother!"

"You tell her to leave," Faith growled.

"It is you! Come here and give your mother-in-law a hug!"

Reece visibly shrank and shuffled across the room for a hug. "Hi, Mrs. A. What brings you here?"

"Oh, Theresa, you could use a shower, dear."

"She just got back from the gym. She likes the gym," Faith mentioned.

Reece stiffened.

"My, you're so tense! Is everything all right?" The older woman stepped back and gave Reece the once over. "You look…well…so big. Do you really think you need to go to the gym so much? "

"Yeah, mom, she's a certified gym rat. And I mean rat." Faith narrowed her eyes at her wife.

Reece narrowed hers back.

Mrs. Ashford looked between them both and raised an eyebrow. "What is going on here?"

Just then the doorbell rang, earning another narrow eyed glare from Reece. Faith opened the door and jumped back.

"*Congratulations!*" Then they started to sing. "For she's a jolly good actress, for she's a jolly good actress, for she's a jolly good actresssssssssss..."

Faith made a frightened face as her mother came to the door. "Mom! You remember Cori and Violet?"

Cori immediately thrust a box behind her back and Violet let go of the balloons she was holding. Reece watched as they floated to the high ceiling and stayed there.

"What's going on? Why are we celebrating?" Marsha asked in excitement.

"Nothing!" Faith blurted.

Cori walked sideways into the kitchen, passing the box to Reece who frowned and opened it. Her eyes widened as a dozen cookies shaped like breasts with one nipple pierced stared back at her. She slammed the box shut just as everybody filed into the kitchen. Putting the box on top of the fridge, she gave Cori an annoyed stare. "We'll just keep them here for now."

Faith shot her wife a questioning look and Reece shook her head.

"Girls, I demand to know what is going on." Marsha had her hands on her hips.

"Well, you see, I am making a movie," Faith started.

"Oh, that's wonderful!"

"Ma, wait, it's a lesbian movie." Faith paused waiting for a reaction.

Marsha cocked her head. "Yes…"

"See, there's some content, some, uh." Faith looked at everyone in the room for help. No one offered.

"What kind of content, dear?"

"Sex, Ma."

Marsha's eyes widened. "Oh. I see." She sat down on a kitchen chair and sucked her lips into her mouth.

The room was dead silent.

Faith sat down across from her mother. "Mom, it's okay, really. It's not porn. It's integral to the story…"

"Yes, I can see where sex is integral to a story," Marsha said sarcastically.

"Mrs. A, if I may," Cori said. "Faith thought long and hard about this and believe me, it was a big issue. She wouldn't do anything embarrassing to you."

"Are you nude?"

Faith swallowed. "A little."

Mrs. Ashford sat in thought. Turning to Reece she looked at her inquisitively.

Reece threw her hands up and shrugged. "Hey, I didn't write it. I have to deal with it, too."

Finding an ally, Marsha nodded at Reece. "I see. And you're all right with this."

"Actually—" Reece began.

Faith cut her off. "Yes, we had a long talk and she's okay with it."

Reece curled her lip. "Yeah, sure."

Marsha wasn't buying it. She'd have to talk to Reece alone.

†

After Cori and Violet left, and Mrs. Ashford was getting unpacked, Faith and Reece sat at opposite sides of their bed and glared.

"I can't believe you took that job! What are you trying to prove?" Faith asked angrily.

"Me? I'm just making a little money," Reece replied innocently.

"Oh, suddenly you're wanting for money?"

Reece stood up. "No, but maybe I want some extra to buy you a present."

Faith stood, too. "Bullshit! You're being spiteful. Don't give me that shit."

Reece stood silently. Was she? She had to be. She had no interest in making more money. Not ready to admit it, she stayed quiet.

With the bed between them they just looked at one another. It was uncomfortable and Reece didn't know how to handle it.

Faith watched as Reece began gathering clothes. "Where are you going?"

"You heard your mother, I stink. I need a shower."

"We're not done yet!"

"I gotta go."

Faith growled and threw herself on the bed. Angry with Reece, she threw her wife's pillows on the floor and stared at them. "Stupid! You're being stupid!" she yelled into the bathroom. Reece closed the door and turned on the shower. Faith sighed and rolled over. Her mother was downstairs, no sense in screaming.

†

Reece let the hot water run on her head. She stood there a long time, not moving, just letting the water run across her ears, her eyes, blocking out sound, blocking out sight. She wanted to stay like that forever, the water drowning out reality. She bent her head, breathing through her mouth. She reached out and leaned both hands on the wall in front of her with her head hung lower. Spite. It was spite. Faith was right. Why else would she set herself up to work with half naked women that she had to touch. After the tirade Faith threw at first mention of the job prospect, it was clear as day she didn't want Reece to do it. *Why?* Reece felt like an ass. Again. *Why do I keep doing this? I don't want to fight with Faith. I don't like how it feels when she's really mad at me. And she is mad. Fuck.*

†

Faith opened the bathroom door silently and looked in. Reece's posture told the story of her thoughts.

She knows she's wrong. Maybe she didn't realize it when she did it, or she wouldn't look so…defeated.

Faith silently left the room and went back to the bed. She sat there and thought about her wife and how she reacted to things. Reece was acting out. She always acted out. Would it be so bad to let her do this training? Reece would never do anything to lose Faith's trust. That was a given. It would also allow Reece the opportunity to feel a sense of satisfaction for herself if she's letting Faith do her thing. Maybe Faith can accept that if she's going to be simulating actual sex with Alicia Alvarez, Reece can train a few women. Fair is fair after all. Isn't it?

†

When Reece finally emerged from her shower, she looked sad. She was surprised to see Faith sitting on the bed. "You're still here?"

Faith smiled. "Come here, sit down."

Reece complied. "Faith, listen, I'm being stupid. I probably did do this out of spite. I don't have to do it. I can call—"

Faith shushed her wife. "No need, baby. You do this. I think you need it. Besides, I'll be gone all the time and you're right. A hobby is a hobby."

131

Reece's jaw dropped. "What just happened when I was in the shower? You were so mad?"

"I thought some." Faith climbed onto her wife's lap and faced her. "I trust you. I was also being selfish. If I'm going to be doing that thing we can't talk about, then why can't you earn a few dollars and get me a present." Faith kissed Reece's nose.

Reece pulled a face. "What's going on?"

Faith laughed softly. "I don't want to fight. Not with you. Not about this."

Reece's face was the picture of relief. "Me neither. I don't want to fight with you."

"The next little while is going to be so stressful for both of us, with me gone more than not, making the movie. You're going to be home obsessing about it. It's going to be hard on us. We need to do things together, not against one another."

Reece's heart burst. "You just said what I was thinking. Are you sure you want me to work at the gym? I don't have to."

"It's fine." Faith kissed Reece's lips. "I have trust and you won't hurt me."

"I try." Reece grinned and looked down. "I can see your tits."

Faith looked down, too. "I should put on clothes now that mom's here. Your shirt doesn't cut it."

Reece wrapped her arm tightly around Faith. "Or you can take that off and we can have make-up sex."

Faith leaned in for a kiss that lasted a long time. She hummed in delight, pressing her body against Reece, letting her weight lean into her. "Tempting, but mom is here."

"I'll be quiet," Reece countered, kissing Faith again, sensuously, convincingly. She held her wife's bottom lip in her teeth and growled playfully.

Faith melted. Groaning, she pushed Reece down onto the bed and resumed the kiss, hard and hot, her libido rising fast. "Mmm, we have to stop. God."

Reece grinned wolfishly. "To be continued?"

"Oh, you bet your ass," Faith replied, swatting said body part as she got off of her wife. "I need to shower, too. Keep mom busy?"

"Thanks a lot," Reece said with a frown.

"I love you, baby."

Reece pursed her lips and started to get dressed.

†

When Faith finished her shower, she came downstairs to find Reece sitting on the couch with Smudge. "I suggest you go look in on mom." She pointed to the kitchen.

Faith, curious, went to do just that. Her eyes bugged out of her head. "Mother! Where did you get that?"

Marsha looked down at her cookie and took a sip of tea. "I was in the mood for a sweet and found these. You know, they're quite good with a cup of tea."

Faith watched as her mother brought the breast shaped cookie with the pierced nipple to her mouth and cringed. "This is wrong on so many levels."

Reece laughed from the living room. "She likes them, Faith."

"Shut up, you."

Reece appeared in the kitchen and opened the box of cookies. She took one out and licked it. "Mmm, sweet."

Faith walked out of the kitchen in a huff, as Reece and Marsha laughed.

†

Reece bit into the cookie and chewed. "You're right, not bad at all."

Mrs. Ashford got up to top off her tea. "Would you like some, dear?"

Reece stood. "No, thanks, I have coffee on."

"Sit, I'll make it for you."

Reece sat. "Thank you."

"So, Theresa, what's really going on with you?"

"What do you mean?"

Mrs. Ashford gave Reece the coffee. "With this movie thing."

Reece sighed. "Faith is an actress, she has a right to do whatever she wants in a movie. I am simply here for support."

"Bullshit. That sounds rehearsed. I know you, young lady."

Reece raised both eyebrows at the older woman's outburst. "Mrs. A, it's not going to be easy for me, but I have to accept it. We fight if I don't."

"A little fight never killed anyone."

Reece slumped in her chair. "I don't want to fight any more. I can't tell her not to. It's her decision."

Mrs. Ashford sighed. "I suppose. She'll only resent you if you force her not to." She sipped her tea and thought. "But sex, on the big screen…how will I survive that?"

"Tell me about it," Reece agreed.

"My husband will have a stroke. I can't tell him this. He'll just die on the spot."

Reece snorted.

"No, Theresa, what will I do?"

Reece shrugged. "I have no idea. Let Faith tell him."

Chapter Ten

Mrs. Ashford decided that the girls just didn't eat right and decided to cook dinner. She drove Reece crazy until she agreed, reluctantly, to take her to the grocery store. While there, Reece pushed the cart while the older woman picked out vegetables.

Reece sighed and shifted from one foot to the other. Shopping wasn't her thing. It never was. Pushing the cart was torture.

"What do you think about this cucumber?" Marsha waved the vegetable in the air in front of Reece.

I can't tell you what I think about that cucumber, Reece thought evilly. "It's okay," she replied, straight faced.

"Good, you girls don't eat enough vegetables. In my day, you ate three square meals, all the food groups were involved. Nowadays, you drive through and buy a burrito to eat while you drive. So unhealthy."

"Mrs. A, we do eat well. I'm always on Faith's case about food."

"Really?" Marsha looked shocked.

"Yeah. I have to eat well to maintain my body weight."

"About that, dear." Mrs. A looked at Reece. "Don't you think you have gone overboard a little bit with the muscles? I mean, it's so butch."

Reece rolled her eyes. "I like it. Faith loves it."

Mrs. Ashford shook her head. "Tell me something. Why would Faith want to do this movie?"

Reece shrugged. "She just wants to."

"I don't understand. It's bad enough the whole world knows her business. Every time you or she is on the cover of a magazine, Quinn is miserable for a week. The men at the lodge stopped talking about it, but he knows what they think. You know, he defends you."

Reece dipped her head in acknowledgement. "That's pretty cool of him."

"You aren't kidding! I never thought he'd come around. But he did, and now this. This is going to push him over the edge. His little girl, doing those things in a movie will be too much... Oh dear, I can't even think about it."

Reece felt very sympathetic. After all, she didn't want to think about it either. She despised the whole idea, but for Faith's sake, tried to show a different outlook. She wished the whole movie would go away. She felt awful when Faith told her they had accepted her changes. She secretly wished they had turned her down and Faith would scrap the whole thing. Life would be so much easier.

Reece tried very hard to seem supportive and she really was, to an extent. She supported Faith's career, even though it put both of them in a very large spotlight on occasion. She wanted her wife to succeed at fulfilling her dreams. It made Faith so happy when she got her first acting job. Reece couldn't love her more when she gushed about it. Now, she almost regretted getting her that first job. Almost. She couldn't regret it entirely.

"Dear?"

"I'm sorry, Mrs. A, I was daydreaming."

"I can imagine what you were thinking. Theresa, honey, can't we talk Faith out of this?"

Reece wished she could. "Nope. I tried. I really tried, but she's very interested in the script as a whole. Besides, she'll hate me if I tell her not to do it."

"But she'll listen if you do."

"Yeah, she will. That's where it gets complicated. I can't forbid her. You just can't do that to a woman like Faith. It'll make her want to do it even more. Look, Mrs. A, I hate it. I hate it more than anything, but I won't tell Faith how much. Let her do it and get it over with. Then we can forget it."

"Someone still has to tell Quinn. Will you?"

Reece screeched to a halt. "No way!"

"I can't tell him and Faith wouldn't dare."

"How do you know? I think Faith should be the one to tell him. After all, she's the one doing it."

Mrs. Ashford nodded. "I think you're right."

†

Quinn Ashford sat back in the chair and smoked his cigar. He loved it when his wife visited the girls. It gave him a chance to sit around in his underwear and smoke his cigars. Marsha made such a fuss about the smell. He grinned and sighed. It was quiet. He liked it, so he made a face when the phone rang. He let the machine answer it and listened to the message.

"Quinn, dear, there's something happening that you're not going to like. I suggest you put out that horrible cigar and call your daughter. Oh, and wash the dishes."

Quinn frowned. What could be going on? It wasn't Reece, that he was certain of. Sure, the club owner was gruff on the outside, but he was convinced she was completely in love with his daughter, and protected her. Boy, did she protect her. He knew it ate her up as much as it ate him up to see a tabloid declaring some lie or another. He knew Reece felt as if she failed to protect Faith from the enemy. It took Quinn a while to accept that Reece had taken up where he left off in taking care of his little girl.

Maybe the girls are fighting. Then again, Marsha would have gotten involved in that and didn't need to tell him. Curious, he stared at the phone.

†

Faith watched sideways while her mother and Reece seemed to become best friends. They chatted as they unpacked the groceries, discussing which way to make the squash. She was very leery as to what happened on their trip to the grocery store. Reece was extremely reluctant to go and now they acted like they were best buddies. Oddly jealous, she started to unpack with them.

"Faith, did your father call?"

"No, Ma, was he supposed to?"

"Hm." Mrs. Ashford began washing vegetables. "He could."

Faith eyed her mother suspiciously. "Mother, did you tell him about the movie?"

Marsha blinked a few times. "Me? Oh, no, you're going to tell him about your little sexcapade you call a movie."

"Mother!" Faith looked to Reece for help and her wife raised her eyebrows and looked away. "Oh, I get it. I get it now. You guys ganged up together. Fast friends with a common agenda. Well, fine!"

Reece shrugged. Mrs. Ashford pursed her lips.

"This isn't fair, Reece. You were supportive of me!"

"I still am. But I don't have to like it."

Faith scowled. "Be that way, the both of you."

Reece smiled. "You're cute when you pout. C'mere."

Faith turned her back. "No. You two be friends. I'll go to Cori's."

Reece panicked. "No, don't go." She went to Faith's side and wrapped an arm around her. "We're just playing. Don't go to Cori's. Okay?"

"Okay, but you'd better be playing."

"I am. I swear."

Mrs. Ashford narrowed her eyes at Reece. "Traitor."

"I have to share a bed with her, Mrs. A." Reece wrapped both arms around her wife and Faith brought her hands up to hold Reece's biceps. "See? She loves my muscles."

"They're so hot," Faith said quietly, but her mother heard her anyway.

"Children, your mother is here."

"Yes, Ma," Faith said, still gripping Reece's arms.

"Besides, I never found all that bulk to be attractive."

"I can tell. Look at Daddy," Faith joked. "He's like a sausage squeezed into polyester."

"Faith Beulah Ashford! That's your father. He does not look like a sausage!"

Reece's body was spasming with silent laughter.

Faith dug her nails into Reece's flesh. "You remember what happened the last time you made fun of my name?"

Reece winced and tried to control herself. "Yes, I do. Beulah is such a lovely name." She snorted and laughed, backing away from her wife.

"Theresa, I hardly find it funny. As I recall, you were named after a nun."

Now Faith laughed. "If she could see you now!"

Reece, properly put in her place, stopped laughing just as the phone rang.

"Faith'll get it."

†

Quinn Ashford had to look everywhere in the house until he found the mess that Marsha called a phone book. Papers shoved inside willy-nilly, nothing under the right letter. Finally finding Faith's number, under T, for Theresa, he began to dial. Feeling apprehensive, he almost hung up. Marsha made him nervous.

"Hello?"

"Faith, honey?"

"Oh, hi, Daddy." Faith cut her eyes at the two women in the kitchen, both standing shoulder to shoulder, watching her intently.

"I got the strangest phone call. Is everything okay?"

"Uh, yeah, why do you ask?" The actress glared outright at her mother and wife, who turned to the sink, looking busy. She could practically see their ears flapping.

"Your mother mentioned something about trouble?"

"Trouble? There's no trouble, where would she get that idea?" Faith walked into the kitchen and pinched her mother.

"Ow! Faith! Is that how you treat your mother?"

"What just happened? Why is she yelling?" Quinn asked, sounding alarmed.

"Nothing, Daddy. Really."

"Faith, are you lying to your father? There's something going on and if I have to come there, I will."

"No! Dad, don't come here." Faith eyed her mother who scowled, rubbing her pinch. Reece shook her head and tsk'd. "Well, actually, there is something I need to tell you. Are you sitting down?"

"Faith, honey, what is it?"

"You see, Dad, I was offered a big part in a movie. The starring role, in fact."

"That's wonderful! What kind of movie is it? Is it a sob story, because you know I can't stomach those movies?"

"No, Daddy." Faith swallowed hard and looked to Reece.

Reece nodded. "You have to tell him before he finds out on his own."

Faith continued, her mouth suddenly dry. "You see, it's a cop movie, and I play one of the cops, and, uhm, it's got some love scenes in it."

"Love scenes? It sounds like a woman's movie. Your mother should love that."

"Actually, Mom isn't all that keen with it." Faith sat down and picked at a placemat. Her mother poked her in the arm. "Those love scenes, are kind of…explicit." Faith waited with her eyes closed. There was no response. "Daddy?"

Quinn cleared his throat. "Well, you're not in them right?"

Faith cringed. "Uh, I am."

Watching her in distress, Reece suddenly began to feel terrible for Faith and stood behind her chair, rubbing her shoulders.

"Oh, I see," Mr. Ashford said quietly.

"Daddy, please, you can start yelling now if you want." Faith felt a soft kiss on her head and closed her eyes again, picturing her father's disapproving face. "Dad?"

"Faith, I don't really know what you expect me to say."

The actress grimaced and Reece squeezed her shoulder. "You can say you hate it."

"I can say that."

Quinn's voice was controlled and Faith knew all about that tone. "Okay, you're not going to say anything. You're just going to keep quiet and make my life miserable by ignoring me, and everything."

"I will not ignore you. I just need time to think. "

There was silence and it made Faith very upset. "Okay. So…do you want to talk to me when you're ready?"

"Just tell me this, is this…explicit sex…with another woman?"

Faith eyed Reece nervously. "Yes, it is with another woman."

"I see. And Reece thinks this is fine?"

"No, she doesn't. Nobody does." The actress became angry. "Everyone hates this but me. I may as well not do this movie if everyone hates it."

"That's your choice. I have to go, Faith."

Faith stared at the table, angry and frustrated, and slammed down the phone. "That went well."

Reece knelt down in front of her wife. "You wanna hit me?"

Faith grinned slightly, "No, baby. I may cry though."

Mrs. Ashford sighed. "You don't have to do the movie, Faith. No one is twisting your arm."

Faith growled and stormed out of the kitchen.

"Mrs. A, the more we tell her not to, the more she will. She's as stubborn as they come."

Marsha sighed heavily. "You know, Theresa, if she's only doing it because we tell her not to, maybe we should encourage her."

Reece pursed her lips in thought. "I dunno. I don't think that will work either. Look, let her do this for whatever reason she needs to."

"But sex, Theresa! I don't know how I can take this!"

"Faith rewrote the scenes, I haven't even seen what she wrote. I have to trust her judgment. She knows this is killing us, but she has a reason to want to do it."

"You're more supportive than her parents."

Reece nodded. "I guess I have to be. I don't like it any more than you do, and as sick as it makes me feel, there's also this other feeling inside, and it tells me I have to let it happen."

Mrs. Ashford's eyes welled up and she sniffed back the tears. "What would she do without you?"

Reece bowed her head in embarrassment.

"No, really. Her father and I can never accept this decision and you of all people can."

Reece sighed. "Don't ask me how."

Faith came back into the kitchen. "Ignore me. I'm just here to get a drink."

"Honey." Mrs. Ashford stood up and opened her arms. "I'm so sorry."

Faith walked into her mother's embrace. "Thank you." She breathed in relief.

Marsha held her daughter at arm's length. "I'm so proud of you and I haven't been showing it at all. I've been acting like such a fool."

"You have no idea what this means to me, Mom."

"I may not be in love with the idea, but honey, this is your movie. I trust you have a good reason to do it. I support you."

Reece smiled as the two women held one another. Now to deal with Faith's father.

Chapter Eleven

Dinner was quiet as everyone had something on their mind. Mrs. A insisted she do dishes and sent the girls out to walk Smudge. It had been quite some time since the two women took a walk together. Every time they went out in public, paparazzi drove them crazy.

Faith attempted to take the leash, but Reece wasn't having it. The actress smiled and watched Reece snap on the leash and scoop the tiny dog up.

"He can walk down the stairs, baby."

Reece bounded down the few steps. "They're too high for his legs."

Faith snickered. "You'd think you gave birth to him."

Reece scowled.

Faith reached up and caressed her wife's cheek. "I think it's utterly adorable."

Reece scowled harder and Faith laughed.

They walked slowly, stopping every so often for Smudge to sniff and lift his leg. Faith smiled to herself, thinking how nice it was to be out without being bothered. She felt completely at ease with Reece by her side, and wished Reece would stop looking over her shoulder every second. "This is nice, for a change."

"They're there, Faith. I know they are."

"Just relax, hold my hand." The actress took the larger hand and squeezed it.

Reece looked down at their hands. "This will be on the cover of the Star tomorrow."

"Fuck 'em. We never have this kind of time together anymore. Just enjoy it."

Reece glanced surreptitiously over her shoulder. Finding it safe, she sighed. "It is nice to hold your hand and not worry about stalkers."

"Think about how nice it would be if you kissed me in public."

Reece raised both eyebrows. "Are you nuts? I know they're there."

Faith growled in frustration. "Reece, you never cared. In the beginning, you couldn't keep your hands or lips off me. Who the hell cares about a stupid tabloid anyway?'

Reece knew Faith was right. She glanced all around before stealing a very quick kiss.

Faith looked amused. "Are you kidding me?

"What? I kissed you."

Faith pushed Reece against a parked car, grabbed her lover's face with both hands and really kissed her. At first Reece resisted, even tried to push Faith off, but as soon as Faith's tongue entered her mouth, she was lost.

Faith groaned, pressing her body against Reece's. Instinctively, two large hands grasped Faith's ass cheeks and pulled her even closer. Faith wrapped her arms around the taller woman's neck. Reece had to admit, it had been a long time since she'd made out with her wife in public and it was exciting. They never used to hide their affection, in fact, they made every effort to show it wherever they were. Suddenly, Reece had an image of herself fucking Faith on her bike and she growled, intensifying the kiss. Lost in their own world momentarily—everything else was gone—no people walking by, no cars blowing their horns, no flashes blinding them.

Flashes? Reece thought hazily. *Flashes!*

Faith jumped back, and Reece lurched forward. In a fit of rage, Reece lunged for the man, ripping his camera from his hands and grabbing him by the shirt.

"Reece! Stop!"

"One fucking night alone! That's all I want, asshole. One fucking night!"

Smudge's leash pulled taut as he tried to run away from the mayhem.

"You're crazy!" the photographer yelled.

Reece realized the leash was around her wrist and she let the man's shirt go, walking up to him, chest to chest. "Now, look! You made me scare my dog!"

"Reece!" Faith grabbed Reece by the arm and tried to pull her back. A barrage of flashes erupted around them.

The furious woman twisted her head around to find that they were surrounded by photographers.

"Gimme my camera, you freak!"

Reece raged, and looked at the camera. As the man grabbed for it, she held it high above her head. "Beg for it, fucker."

The paparazzi went wild.

"Reece! That's enough! Give him the damned camera!"

Reece looked at Faith and saw fear. "Fucking hell!" She threw the camera at the trembling man and growled. "Get the fuck away from us!" She turned around and pointed at the other photographers. "Fuck off!" Reece was trying her hardest not to strangle everybody. She was trembling with the squelching effort.

Faith saw the shiver and acted. She took hold of her dangerously angry wife by the arm and yanked her hard. "Let's go. *Now!*"

Reece growled one last time and allowed Faith to drag her away.

"What the hell was that all about? Reece! You don't want to be front page? Well, you just made front page!"

"Fuck them! All I want is to be able to walk in the street with you!"

Faith ignored the outburst, and continued to drag her reluctant lover home. She was pissed also, but Reece was downright shaking. It wasn't normal. It was natural for Reece to be annoyed, angry even, but she was livid tonight.

"Stupid photographers. I hate this! I really hate this, Faith!"

Faith grabbed Reece by both arms and turned her so they were facing one another. "Oh, and you think I like this? It comes with the territory. I'm an actress. A lesbian actress with a big scary wife who owns a tit club! We're freaks, Reece, and people love to pay to watch freaks! Deal with it!"

Reece watched open mouthed as her wife stormed off down the block. Shaking her head, she scooped up Smudge and took off after her. "Wait, Faith, don't run off alone!"

"Leave me alone, Reece, please."

Reece followed Faith until she was safely inside the house. "What the fuck just happened to my Faith?" she asked the dog. "All I wanted was one night alone. I just wanted to hold her hand and walk like a normal couple. Left alone."

✝

Faith slammed the door behind her, startling her mother.

"Honey?"

"Mom, please. Don't."

Mrs. Ashford followed Faith anyway. "What just happened? Where's Theresa?"

"I don't really care." Faith tried to close the bedroom door, but her mother barged through.

"You are going to tell me what happened," the older woman insisted.

"Mom! I really don't—"

"Is it the movie?"

Faith blew out a frustrated, groaning sound. "Yes. Everything is about the movie. Everything."

"Well, then don't you think you may want to rethink this whole idea? There are plenty of movies to do. You don't have to do this one."

Faith bit her tongue so as not to swear at her mother.

They both heard Reece come in. Faith turned her back, and Mrs. Ashford went downstairs.

†

"Theresa, what happened?"

"Photographers. Stupid photographers."

"I'm sure if you just stood still and posed for them they'd have no bad things to say and they'd stop following you. You wouldn't be chased so much."

"We did that. We tried that. It didn't work. All I wanted was peace and quiet to kiss my wife!"

"Theresa, dear, everything has changed now."

"No kidding. I think I just made everything so much worse, too. I went ape-shit on the guy and more freaking photographers jumped out of the woodwork and got pictures of me flipping out."

"Oh, no!"

"Yeah." Reece said with remorse. "Big bad dyke beats up photographer."

Mrs. Ashford rubbed Reece's arm. "I'm sorry this happened tonight. I know it's been so stressful lately. Why don't you girls go away somewhere?"

"I'd love that, but Faith has a movie meeting tomorrow."

"Oh."

Reece sat in thought for a while. A slew of emotions crossed her features. "I gotta get ready for work."

†

Faith didn't move when Reece entered the room. "It's behind the door."

Reece looked behind the door and found her tux hanging. "Thanks."

It was tense. Reece hated it. She was already tense and didn't appreciate her wife creating more tension. She quickly dressed and left for work.

Chapter Twelve

Sarge wasn't surprised to see her boss storm past her. It was a normal occurrence these days. She shook her head in sadness, wishing she could help with her problems, but she couldn't. However, she could count on Cori to be there always to help. Then again, sometimes the blue haired dancer made more trouble than there already was. Sarge thought, how much worse could it get? It was worth a shot. She waited impatiently for Cori to arrive.

†

Reece slammed the heavy door to her office and sank down in her big leather chair. Throwing her feet on the desk hard, she cursed out loud. *Why was all this happening?* Finally finding the love of her life, finally letting love in, and it was all of a sudden so complicated. Everything was so right, it was getting so comfortable. Then this. The television show wasn't so bad, Faith only had to kiss a guy. Reece thought how upset she been about that and chuckled dryly. Shit, that was nothing compared to this.

I'd rather have her kiss a million guys than to touch Alicia Alvarez.

She buzzed the intercom to the front bar, hoping the bartender would see the flashing light. She waited, and waited, then slammed her feet on the floor. The last thing she wanted tonight was to pretend to be pleasant to the customers. Making her way through the crowd with a big scowl on her face, she blew behind the bar, growling at the poor busy bartender, and reaching into her private stash. It was a no alcohol club, but Reece always had a stash for herself.

†

Faith grumped around the house, avoiding her mother well enough until the older woman went to bed. She thought about her father and how he was going to take this whole thing. He'd be upset, he already was and she'd expected that. It's not like she was seeking approval from him, or from her mother for that matter. If that were the case, she'd be married to some stockbroker and living on Long Island with two kids by now. But it still hurt to have her father disappointed. She knew he was. She could hear him now…he didn't raise her to be having sex on a screen for everyone to see. Her mother was just as upset, but, bless her, she was trying to accept the decision. Reece. Now that hurt her the most.

Surely Reece was capable of understanding this was just play-acting, she wasn't a moron. She's just playing the part of one. Faith was sure Reece knew in her heart Faith wasn't doing this just to hurt her. Reece just had a different way of coping. Faith grimaced. Reece was completely enraged earlier, and seemed to swallow the anger dry. It was bubbling inside of her. It wouldn't take much of anything to set her off and Lord help the poor person who did it.

Faith knew it wouldn't be her but she would feel the wrath for some time until Reece let it out. She shook her head and sighed. Tomorrow morning she'd sit with the presumed cast to have some sort of a meeting. She'd probably have to come face to face with Alicia. A lot of mixed emotions surfaced. *This was going to be something.*

†

Sarge met Cori halfway down the stairs to the club and dragged her off to the side.

"Whassup?" Cori wondered.

"What's going on with Reece?"

"Oh, please. It's a long drawn out project. Why? Is she here already?"

"Yeah, and she's in one hell of a mood."

Cori frowned. "Shit. They must have had another fight."

"Faith?"

"Yeah, and Faith's mom is there so they really can't have it out. It's this movie. I'll see what I can do."

"Thanks, Cor. I knew you'd at least try."

Cori laughed. "Yeah, I must be a bit suicidal, but hell, I love that pain in the ass."

She knocked on the closed office door, not expecting a response. She didn't expect the door to be unlocked either, but amazingly, it was. Reece was sitting at her desk, shoulders slumped, her hands wrapped around a bottle of Jack Daniels. Cori knew Reece was aware of her. "Hey," she said quietly. "The door was open."

Reece gave her a tight-lipped half smile. "I was expecting you."

"And you still left it open?" Cori closed the door behind her and sat on the desk.

Reece blew out a loud breath. "Really, Cor, would you have ever stopped knocking?"

"No. So," Cori nodded toward the bottle. "I thought I was a better friend than Jack."

"Jack doesn't ask questions."

"True. Jack doesn't care about you like I do. Talk to me."

"No."

"Reece, you left the door open, talk."

Reece gritted her teeth. "It's hard. You just won't get it."

"Try me. I'm smarter than I look."

Reece swung her chair around and jumped out of it. She began pacing. "I just want things back to normal! I don't want cameras and magazines, and autographs. I don't want tabloid assholes sneaking into my club and fucking everything up. I just want it back the way it was! Is that so hard to understand?"

"No, it's not."

"Then why is Faith so fucking mad at me? She blew a fit tonight like she never did before. I feel like she's not the same Faith. I want it all to go away."

Cori pursed her lips in thought. This wasn't easy for Reece to hear and she wanted to choose her words carefully.

Reece took a big swallow of whiskey and made a sound as it burned.

"Reece, you can't go backward. You can only go forward, the both of you together. You can't be at one another's throats or it will destroy you."

Reece scowled. "Faith already hates me."

"No, she doesn't and you know that. She hates the way you're acting. You're being unreasonable."

Reece blew up. "See! I knew you didn't get it!"

"Then leave. If it's so hard to accept Faith's profession and the details that come with it, leave her."

Reece's eyes widened. "Fuck off, Cori."

Cori was up in Reece's face. "Then deal with it. Like the fucking adult that you are."

Reece's nostrils flared. "I can't."

"Yes, you very well can. She's gonna do this movie, and you're gonna deal with it."

"I sure am," Reece said, swallowing another mouthful of liquor.

Cori poked Reece in the shoulder. "Yeah, drunk and stupid."

"My choice, and don't poke me again."

"Or what? Reece you don't need this and Faith doesn't either. So, you'll forget about it for one night, but it'll still be there in the morning. The last thing we all need is you drunk and out of control."

"I'm all by myself. I'm perfectly in control and if you're so worried about me, I'll just stay here tonight."

"Oh, sure, that'll make everything better."

Reece growled. "Isn't it time you got out of here?"

"I'm going. Just remember Faith loves you with every breath in her body. She's not doing anything other than what she always dreamed of doing. Don't take it away from her. She'd never do that to you."

†

Faith saw who it was on the caller ID and didn't pick up the phone. She knew Cori was going to try to appeal to her common sense and Faith didn't want to think with common sense. She just wanted to go through the script and prepare for the morning. She briefly wondered if something happened with Reece, but if it did, she knew Cori would be more adamant and not hang up. Sighing, she grimaced as the phone rang again. She tried to ignore it but Cori was being persistent.

"What?"

"I know you know why I'm calling."

"Yeah, she's miserable, isn't she?"

"Beyond. Cut her some slack, Faith. This is hard for her."

"I have cut her some slack. She's being impossible now."

"She's drinking, babe. Just a heads up."

"Thanks, Cori. I gotta go."

"I don't like this at all. I love you both but you're going to give me an ulcer. Just chill, already."

Faith felt guilty. "I'm sorry, Cor. I love you, too. Thanks for trying to talk sense into me. And thank you even more for letting me know that she is drowning her sorrows."

"You're welcome. Now, I'm the one that's gotta go."

Faith scowled at the dial tone and reached for the dog. "So, she's getting drunk huh? She's going to want to come home and make love. Reward herself for drinking. Well, not tonight. She needs to realize that making love isn't always the answer."

†

Reece was pretty drunk by the time she left The Lounge, but no one was able to tell. She was really good at hiding her intoxication when it counted. She made her way out into the early morning air and took a deep breath. She began walking up the avenue, deciding to take advantage of the almost empty streets. Just as she made it two blocks, she felt them behind her. Her hackles bristled.

"Hey, that's a chick in that tuxedo."

Reece smiled evilly. Come on, boys, say it.

She heard snickers of laughter behind her, conspiratorial whispers and her evil grin became wider.

"I know. It's a friggin' dyke."

Make me turn around. Come on, fuckers. You have no idea what you're doing.

"Hey, dyke, wanna meet a real man?"

Reece spun around in a flash, her fist connecting solidly with flesh and bone.

He hit the ground on his ass. One boy ran, the other stood, stunned.

"Come on, dickhead, make me hit you again." She advanced on the guy and he tried to scoot back as his friend was trying to pick him up. His friend went down behind him.

"You fucking broke my nose, you dyke bitch!" Blood sprayed from his mouth as he yelled.

Reece's eyes flashed and gave the kid a glimpse of The Animal lurking beneath the surface. She yanked him up violently by the sleeve, cocking back her fist. "There's plenty more where that came from. Wanna try me?"

The kid pissed himself and Reece laughed. "Stupid boy, go home before I really hurt you." She released him and he almost killed himself trying to run away.

Reece groaned loudly. That felt way too good. It would take hours to compose herself before getting home.

†

Faith felt her wife in the room although she didn't hear her sneak in. She sensed Reece standing behind her, and if she concentrated, she could hear her breathing. "I see you finally made it home. What time is it? Oh, it's seven. Good morning."

Reece was surprised to see Faith dressed so early. She wanted to crawl in bed and make love. She walked to where Faith was facing and knelt down in a wobbly fashion. "Where are you going?"

Faith wrinkled her nose. "You're drunk."

"So?"

"I have a meeting, remember?"

"Yeah, but, I want you."

"You should have thought about that before you came stumbling home at seven."

"Kiss me," Reece demanded leaning forward.

Faith watched her wife fall against her knees. "Charming. I gotta go. The car is waiting for me."

Reece looked toward the shadow that just appeared next to her and tried to scramble to her feet.

"Theresa. Good morning."

"Morning," Reece mumbled and went after Faith. "Baby, I just needed to forget!"

"I'll call you later." Faith slipped into the big black car and was gone.

Reece leaned against the doorframe, her mouth feeling dry and hot. She scowled and made her way to the fridge for some water.

"So, you are drunk."

"Don't you start with me, too. I'm going to bed."

Mrs. Ashford felt horrible for Reece. She wanted to hug her, but didn't know if she could. "Faith told me you have some new job at the gym, do you want me to wake you?"

"Shit!" Reece blurted. "I forgot about that. Yeah, please wake me at noon."

Her daughter's wife looked so sad, and wounded as she trudged up the stairs. Marsha took a deep breath and made her way to the sofa, Smudge hot on her heels. She patted the small dog on the head and flipped on the television. This was going to be a long morning.

Chapter Thirteen

Faith slumped into the back seat of the car. Ted glanced at her in the rear view mirror and frowned. "Are you okay, Miss Faith?"

"Quit calling me 'Miss Faith', Mr. Williams."

Ted chuckled. "You know she would kill me. She insists I address you with respect."

Faith frowned. "Yeah, well, she isn't here."

The driver grinned, glad Reece wasn't there to glare at him every time he blew through a yellow light. "Why so sad? You should be excited."

"I am excited, trust me," Faith replied flatly.

Ted shook his head.

Faith sat in silence the rest of the way, thinking a myriad of things.

Is Reece sleeping? Is she even home? Will she even be there later? When is mom leaving? When will dad start speaking to me again? What is Alicia really like? How does she kiss? Are her lips dry? How will Reece react when the sex scenes arrive? How will I feel when I kiss Alicia? What if I get hot?

"We're here, Miss Faith."

Faith blinked a few times before realizing they had stopped. "Oh, thanks. I don't know how long I'll be."

"That's all right, I'll be around when you're ready."

Faith stood in front of the building with excitement and trepidation.

Well, here goes nothing.

†

Faith's sharp nails bit painfully into Reece's overheated flesh as she pumped into her. The actress's heels dug into her lower back, pulling her deeper inside with every thrust. Reece sweated with the effort, grunting with every movement of her hips. Faith's mouth was open, little breathy sounds of pleasure escaping, driving Reece deeper into her sexual haze.

"Come for me, Faith."

"Oh, yes…" Faith breathed out.

Reece bit her bottom lip, hard, as she watched the extent of Faith's pleasure wash across her face. "Come on, baby," she encouraged.

Faith dug into Reece harder, with her legs and nails, throwing her head back.

"That's it, Faith—"

Faith groaned deeply. "Ohhhh, Alicia!"

Reece woke immediately, with a loud growl. "What the fuck kind of dream is that?" She asked the empty room. "Fuck!" Her head pounded.

Was that what Faith was thinking? Sometimes, she wouldn't open her eyes, even after Reece told her to.

The quiet knock on the door made her pull the covers up over her sweaty body. "Yeah, Mrs. A, I'm up."

Marsha opened the door and looked in. "Oh, dear, Theresa! Look at you! Did you have a nightmare?"

"Oh, yeah, a horrible one," Reece muttered, rubbing her red eyes.

"Would you like to talk about it?"

"No. Thanks for waking me. I gotta get ready."

The older woman watched Reece skeptically for a moment, then left.

†

It took forever for everyone to arrive. Faith looked around at all the people and couldn't help noticing that Alicia was constantly staring at her. Deciding to make the first move, Faith walked to her, extended her hand, and smiled warmly.

"Hi, I'm Faith Ashford."

Alicia scanned Faith up and down. "I know who you are."

Faith withdrew her hand, feeling stupid.

Alicia's expression of boredom never changed. "So, we have to roll around like two dogs in heat, huh? I sure hope you shower."

Faith's eyes widened in shock. "Excuse me?"

"You know and brush your teeth."

Faith's mouth hung open. *Why that little bitch!*

"Yeah, I never kissed a girl before. I know you have. Shit the world knows you're a big time lesbo. Frankly, I don't get it. Women hit on me all the time. I mean I know I'm hot, but really, don't go falling in love with me after one kiss. And don't think you're going to convert me. I like dick too much."

Faith finally found her voice. "Did anyone ever tell you that you're a bitch?"

Alicia studied her nails. "Yes."

Faith growled under her breath. "You have got to be kidding! I have no intentions of converting you. You're the one that better be careful because after one kiss from me, you'll be the one begging for more, and let me tell you something, you better shower too because believe it or not, your shit does stink!" Faith walked away in an aggravated huff. *Of all the stupid cocky snobs!*

†

Reece downed two aspirin with her giant cup of coffee and by the time she got to the gym, her head had stopped throbbing. Still, she didn't feel like working out herself, but figured showing a few lame beginners the ropes wouldn't be too hard on her. The staff shirt they gave her now sported cut off sleeves and bottom. She figured they wouldn't care as long as the word *staff* was still there. Checking in at the desk, the receptionist told to wander around and ask clients if they were interested in a personal trainer.

Scanning the area, she spotted so many women and men using the equipment improperly—using too much weight, not enough weight, standing wrong, and so on. She sighed deeply. Never really watching anyone else before, she couldn't believe how stupid people were. Folding her arms, she wandered around, not knowing where to start.

She didn't have to wait long. As she was standing in the middle of the gym, a woman came to her. Reece looked at the young woman, maybe twenty, or so and rolled her eyes. There wasn't an ounce of fat on her and she apparently knew it by the clothes she was hardly wearing. She had a flat stomach, perfectly round ass, and great legs. It figures, I'd have to touch her. "You need some help?"

"I think so. My name is Jennifer. So you work here?"

Reece nodded. "Yeah. What do you need help with?"

"My legs, they're so fat!"

Reece's eyebrows jumped. Fat? Where the hell did she see fat?

The girl must have read her mind because she slapped her own inner thighs. "Here? Don't you see?"

"Oh, okay. So, do you want to build muscle there?" Reece asked nervously.

Jennifer perked right up. "Sure! Can you do that?"

"For a fee, yeah."

"Okay, show me what to do!"

Reece sighed. She hoped the girl would do two squats and give up. She walked her into the weight room. "Okay, you need to stretch first, have you done that yet?"

Jennifer shook her head.

Reece pointed to a mat. "Lay down and pick up your leg." Reece took the girl's foot and began to stretch her leg. The girl was wearing a tiny sports bra and the mat must have been cold because her nipples hardened. Reece tried to look away, but couldn't. *Shit.* Not knowing what to do, the normally quiet Reece began to talk. "So, you'll have to stretch all the time before you work out so remember what I'm doing. Gimme the other leg."

Reece tried to think about anything but this girl's well-shaped breasts with what looked to be great nipples. "Have you ever done squats?"

"No, will you show me?"

Great. This is just great. I'm fucking horny for days, and now this.

†

Faith shook her head adamantly. "No, I won't do it. She's an obnoxious bitch!"

The director insisted. "You two have to get comfortable with one another or nothing on screen will be believable. You don't have to sleep with her, just spend time with her."

"She's impossible!"

"So. I can't have that kind of tension between the two leading ladies."

Faith scowled. "Lunch, that's all I agree to."

"Fine." He waved Alicia to him. "You two are going to sit there and get to know one another, got it?"

Alicia grinned. "Haven't you been reading the tabloids? I know all I need to know about her."

"Just do it." The director walked away.

Faith narrowed her eyes. "Look, you are on my last nerve, and I really don't know how we're going to pull this off, but we have to, so shut up and let's go pretend to like one another."

Alicia shrugged. "I don't know about you, but I'm an actress and I can make anything work."

Faith threw her hands in the air. "Are you insinuating I'm not an actress? Fuck you!"

Alicia laughed. "You'd love that, wouldn't you?"

Faith nearly screamed. "I can't believe I ever thought nice things about you! You are the worst!"

"You thought about me?"

"Yes, I did. I thought nasty, hot, sweaty, lesbian thoughts about you," Faith said with a smirk.

Alicia appeared sick. "Ew!"

"Naked, writhing, body twisted, screaming thoughts." Faith nearly guffawed at Alicia's expression. "Now, don't you think it's time we got to know one another better?"

Alicia's eyes bugged out. "You're going to get all turned on kissing me! You have to do things with me…sexual things! Oh, my God!"

Faith grinned widely. "Yep. You up for it, big mouth? I mean, a lesbo like me is only after one thing. Right?"

"Are you fucking with me, Faith?"

"Maybe. I suppose you'll just have to keep wondering what I'm thinking at every turn."

†

Reece was in hell. She wanted to scream. She barely had time to recover from touching Jennifer's inner thighs when another, even more attractive girl needed her assistance. Her libido, already on high alert for days, made her very uncomfortable in her shorts. She wavered between horny and angry as her dream kept popping back into her head all day. Each time Faith called out Alicia's name, Reece went crazy inside. Usually when that happened, she'd focus on the girl she was training and get hot and bothered. Then she'd feel guilty, think about Faith, and the whole cycle started again. To top things off, her aspirin had stopped working a long time ago and her head was throbbing again.

Irrationally, she wanted a piece of Alicia Alvarez. A tooth would be nice. She wore a feral grin, imagining herself knocking out that tooth. Sure, she knew it wasn't Alicia's fault, but still, who could she hit? She had to hit somebody, if only in her fantasies. She'd gotten lucky no one was there to see her beat that boy. Reece was not at all ready to go to jail again, but it would feel so good to hurt someone right now. Having nowhere else to turn, she walked quickly to the heavy bag and let it all go.

†

Faith quickly tired of playing with Alicia and took a good look at her. Her skin was smooth and practically flawless, her lips full and sexy. Her dark hair was pulled back into a loose ponytail, and her body was to die for. Faith could see what had attracted her in the first place. Until she opened her cocky little mouth. Faith shook her head in disappointment. What a waste of good looks. As long as Alicia stuck to the lines, Faith figured it wouldn't be too hard to make the scenes believable. She hoped it would, because no matter how good looking she was, Alicia Alvarez was damned ugly.

"Why are you staring at me?"

Faith rolled her eyes. "Don't worry, I'm not fantasizing."

"Then why are you staring?"

"Tell me, why did you take this movie?" Faith wondered.

"The exposure. You lesbos are always drooling about me on those stupid web pages, and face it, homos are a big deal nowadays."

"I see. But how did you think you'd be able to do these rather intense love scenes with another woman if you think it's so disgusting?"

"I said I'm an actress, a damned good one. I'll imagine you have a big dick and hairy chest. You should be kissing my ass that I'm in this little low budget film. I'll bring the audience that would never even dream of going to a homo movie."

Faith sat back in her chair. "Did anyone ever tell you what a pleasure it is talking to you?"

The dark haired actress snickered. "Look, you don't have to like me, but what I just said is true. I'll bring you exposure you'd never have had without me."

Faith frowned. She was right. "I don't know how you'll pretend I have a dick when you have to touch my tits," she said with a grin.

"I don't either, but I'm sure I'll think of something." She looked directly at Faith's chest. "Hmm, they're pretty big. I suppose I could pretend I'm sucking on a cantaloupe."

Faith sighed. This was going to be one hell of an experience. She no longer worried about kissing Alicia and getting hot. Now she worried about getting nauseous.

†

Cori laughed into the phone. "She said what?"

Faith growled. "It's not funny! She asked me how I could live without a fat juicy dick. Can you even imagine?"

Cori laughed harder.

"Yeah, you laugh. I have to make out with this bitch. I have to suck her tongue without vomiting."

Cori calmed down. "Aw, babe, relax. Just think, you used to want to make out with her."

"Yeah, well, that's a faded memory."

"Besides that, how'd it go?"

"It went great. Everyone is so great. We read through a few things as a group and it seems like we'll all do fine. Except for Alicia. All she can talk about is how hot she is."

Cori snickered. "You gotta admit, she is hot."

"I don't like her any more. You know, I used to worry about getting turned on when we interacted, now I worry I won't pull it off. Cor, there's a point where she's gotta lick my tit, it's like a split second on the screen, but that scene itself will probably be the worst torture for the both of us. Not that I care how bad it is for her."

Cori listened to Faith laugh evilly and grinned. Now that the hard stuff was done and Faith wouldn't be getting hot for Alicia, a whole new can of worms had opened up.

"Cor, with everything that's been going on today, I can't stop worrying about Reece. She was in a state this morning and I was pretty abrupt with her. I felt guilty all day."

"So, make it up to her tonight," Cori said in a teasing voice.

"Hmmm. You know, it has been a while and she is cute when she's horny."

The dancer giggled. "Faith's gonna get some. Faith's gonna get some."

"If she's not too angry with me. She's been so hard to handle lately."

"Oh, I'm sure you can handle anything she brings your way."

Faith smiled. "You bet. I gotta go, they're calling me back."

†

Reece was dying to get out of there. Women surrounded her, everywhere, wanting to touch her muscles, wanting her to touch theirs. Her head was exploding, her stomach was growling, and she was incredibly horny. She was sweaty and hot and wanted to leave. First, she had to work out schedules for these women, all of them. Right now, she was angry and frustrated, but knew training these women would keep her damned busy while Faith was filming. She took out her planner from her duffle bag and began making appointments.

175

Finally, out on the street, Reece took a deep breath and savored the fresh air. She took another breath and tried to center herself. First, she needed a shower and then she needed food. She was in a very cranky mood, and people weren't on her list of things to deal with, but Faith's mom was in the house. She was frustrated on so many levels, and wasn't certain she could be civil to the older woman. Choosing her destination, Reece headed toward the club, where she had a shower and a change of clothes always waiting for her.

†

Faith returned home, ready to explode with all the information she had to share. Finding the house empty was a relief and annoying at the same time. It was a relief, because her mother may have gone home, annoying because she had no one to tell the day's events to. She wouldn't call Reece, she could be in the middle of training someone, and she didn't want to interfere. This wouldn't be a two-minute phone call—she had a lot to say. She looked down and grinned. The house wasn't completely empty; Smudge was bouncing around saying hello. She picked him up, and after what seemed like a million happy kisses, took him to the recliner and leaned back.

"Looks like you and me, bud. Let me tell you what happened today with that bitch Alicia."

†

Reece felt a little more human after she'd cleaned up and eaten something. Still, she was really preoccupied with thoughts of Faith having sex with Alicia. It ate her the hell up. Faith was hers, and she didn't share well with others— especially her wife. Reece knew she had to snap out of this dark mood, or someone was going to get hurt, but she couldn't. She just couldn't think about anything else. Seeing no relief, she decided to stay in her office, away from danger.

†

After finding the note her mother left, saying that she went home, Faith immediately called Reece. She was disappointed when the voicemail came on, but left the good news. She eventually went up to bed, hoping Reece would be home when she woke up. When she did awaken, it was early in the morning, and Reece had not come home. She knew this because Smudge slept by the front door all night waiting for her. Now, angry, Faith dialed Reece's cell phone again.

†

Reece had turned off her cell phone last night after several of the women she was to train kept calling. It didn't matter to them that Reece said she was married, these girls were persistent, and with Reece already in a destructive mood, she opted for turning off the phone. She didn't even think about Faith trying to reach her, assuming Faith would know where she was when she didn't show up at home. She was far too agitated to go home, afraid she'd be horrible to Faith, and it wasn't her fault.

Sleeping in her office was nothing new to her. The couch was comfortable, but it wasn't home and she woke up pretty much in the same mood she went to sleep in. Her cell phone began to ring the moment she turned it on. At first, she growled at the phone until she noticed it was Faith. Then she grimaced. She thought about letting the voice mail take it, but knew that Faith would show up if she didn't answer. She reluctantly pressed the button. "Yeah."

†

Faith heard that tone and sighed. "So, how long are you going to hide out at your club?"

Reece shrugged. "Dunno. Why?"

"Why? Because you're my wife and I want to see you."

"Faith, I'm in no mood right now."

Faith was trying to keep her anger in check. "You just can't keep running off every time things get too thick for you. You need to stop that shit already."

"I don't think you need to be in my company," Reece said tersely.

"Shut the hell up, Reece. I don't care what mood you're in, I don't care at all. I love you and expect to see you here soon. Besides, Smudge is miserable."

"But your mother—"

"Is gone. She left because she thought we needed some alone time. Now cut the crap and get home."

Reece groaned. "Faith, please…"

Frustrated, Faith nearly yelled. "You know…do what you want. I'm leaving in a couple of hours. If I see you, I see you."

Chapter Fourteen

Faith wasn't fooling herself thinking Reece would come home. She knew better, and she also knew better than to go to the club and confront her wife. She sighed and sat down in the recliner with Smudge. She petted the dog as she made herself even more angry, thinking about how when she really needed Reece, she'd run off. Suddenly her hackles rose and she looked around. She felt like someone was watching her and found the photographer peeking out from between two cars. His long lens aimed right at her. She gave him the finger and shut the blinds properly. She thought about what might have happened to that man had Reece been home and grinned.

My big bad protector. My hero.

She smiled. She missed Reece terribly and wanted to be wrapped up in those strong arms.

Not in the mood for glamour, Faith threw on sweats and a baggy shirt. She was tying her sneakers when the phone rang. Thinking it was Reece, she answered it before the second ring.

"Louise! How's it hanging?"

Faith smiled instantly. "John, you big Mary. Am I going to see you today?"

"But of course. Listen, I have big juicy gossip that you just need to hear."

Faith sat down, knowing John's gossip could go on for days. "So, what is it?"

"Rumor has it in hair and makeup that they're going to ambush you and miss bitchy panties into doing a nudie scene today!"

Faith jumped up. "*What*? I didn't prepare! I need time to mentally deal with that little shit! God, I didn't shave my legs!"

John laughed his ass off. "That's the point. They know how famously you two get along and wanted to throw you both into it without warning so there's no time to think."

"Holy shit." Faith was silent as a million things ran through her head.

"Hellooooo...Did you swoon on me? Don't bruise yourself. I'm not sure I have enough cover-up."

"No, I'm here. Shit. Okay, listen I gotta go. I need to shave. Everything."

John chuckled. "Don't rush, honey, I don't want you showing up with little bloody bits of toilet tissue on you."

Faith smiled despite her anxiety. "Yes, ma'am."

After she hung up the phone with John, Faith called Cori and Violet, gave their voice mail the short story, and ran to the bathroom to strip herself of hair.

†

Reece sulked around the office, debating whether or not to go home when Faith was there, or after she left. Finally making a decision, she headed home, with the excuse that Smudge needed her. Finding the house empty was a relief and a disappointment. She was glad that Mrs. A was gone, but disappointed because she had missed Faith.

All her procrastinating just made it worse on her when Faith came home later. Reece made her way upstairs, to gather gym clothes for training, and on seeing the mess that used to be the bathroom, she wondered what was going on. With Smudge hot on her heels, she didn't have time to stand there and stare. She quickly scooped up her dog and after a myriad of happy kisses, took him for a walk.

†

Cori took a sip of coffee as she checked her messages and nearly spit it on the kitchen floor. "Vi!"

Violet came running into the kitchen, half naked. "What? What happened?"

182

"Faith's doing the sex today!"

Violet's eyes widened. "Today? The first thing they film? How can they do that?"

"John heard a rumor and Faith just conveyed. Man, imagine being Faith."

"Imagine being Reece?" Violet countered.

Cori made a face. "Yeesh. I better go soothe the savage beast."

†

Reece dressed in her gym clothes, and was just about to leave when the doorbell rang. Making an annoyed face, she yelled in her most menacing voice. "Who?"

"Me, Reece, you gotta open up, it's really important!"

Reece closed her eyes and took a breath. She wasn't in the mood at all to hear another one of Cori's dissertations about how to treat Faith. She took her gym bag and keys, preparing to walk right past the dancer.

Cori jumped back as Reece barreled through the front door. "Where are you going?"

"Gym. I got training." Reece couldn't help noticing the new addition to Cori's already freaky body. "Nice hair. When did you do that?" Reece pointed to the new labret piercing.

"Last night, and thanks. I think this color pink is delicious." Cori primped her hair.

"If you like cotton candy. Look, I gotta go. Someone is waiting for me."

Cori hurried to keep up with the long strides of her friend. "Reece, do you have any idea where Faith is?"

Reece shrugged. "At the studio?"

"Yes, and do you know what she's doing?"

Reece stopped and pinned Cori with a look. "Cori, I don't have time for games. Spit it out."

Cori hated being pinned by those ice blue eyes, especially now when she had to tell Reece the news. "Faith and Alicia are doing a sex scene today."

Reece swallowed hard. "What?"

"Yeah, John told Faith and now she's freaking out. I just thought you might want to know."

Reece felt like her head might explode. "Oh."

Cori held Reece by her forearm. "You knew this was coming and if you ask me, despite your immature attitude, you should have been there for her this morning."

Reece narrowed her eyes. "Are we quite done?"

"Yes." Cori released the arm. "Don't go doing anything stupid."

"Whatever."

Cori watched Reece head toward her bike and took a deep breath. "For Faith's sake, just go to the gym."

Reece straddled her bike, put her helmet on, and took off.

†

Reece's head was swimming and it wasn't conducive to driving. She pulled to the side and hit the kickstand hard. Closing her eyes and throwing her head back, she took several deep breaths and tried to think clearly. Right now, Faith could possibly be naked with Alicia. This was not sitting well with Reece at all. Her heart was pounding in her ears and her stomach felt sick. This was not good.

Her instinct was to drive right to the studio and stop it from happening, but her rational mind knew better. The problem was, her irrational impulse was so much stronger, and she struggled to stay in control. Her cell phone began to ring, snapping Reece out of her daze. She cursed as she answered.

"Reece? Is that you?"

Puzzled, Reece cocked her head. "Yeah, who's this?"

"Jennifer. We had an appointment at the gym a half hour ago. Are you coming?"

Reece squeezed her eyes shut tightly and pinched the bridge of her nose. Faith, Jennifer, Faith, Jennifer…Her stomach cramped. "No, I have an emergency, I have to cancel today."

"Oh. I understand. Should I tell the desk?" The disappointment was clear in Jennifer's voice.

"Please, look, I gotta go." Reece closed her phone and narrowed her eyes. Faith it was.

†

Faith zipped out of the black car, leaving Ted to chuckle to himself about her nerves. The actress had complained non-stop about Alicia and having to pretend to like the woman. Ted had no idea what to expect from Miss Faith when he picked her up later.

The actress ran right to the make-up room and jumped on John. "Tell me, what exactly did you hear?"

John laughed. "Calm down, honey! Sit, let me fix this bird's nest."

Faith ran a hand through her hair. "It's fine, now talk."

"Well, Alicia seems to have heard the same rumor and is making like it's no big deal. However, my sources tell me she's a nervous wreck about her first kiss with a woman."

"Aw, the poor baby." Faith made a face. "I hope she hurts herself worrying."

"Meow!" John made scratching gestures. "Anywho, just listen to me. All you have to do is close your eyes and pretend it's your Amazon of a wife."

"John, it's not that easy. I don't like Alicia. She's a cow and she said my tits are like melons."

The make-up artist studied Faith's breasts. "What kind of melons."

"John! Did you hear what scene?" Faith asked nervously, while John pulled out a make-up brush.

"Didn't you take a look around? There's a police car in the back. They made it look like night."

Faith paled. "That scene?"

"Mm, hmm." John hummed. "Girl, where the hell did you get these dark circles?"

"Never mind my bags. That scene is probably the hottest one!"

"Oooo, yay! That means I get to see your titties!"

"See them? Alicia's going to taste them." Faith covered her chest with her hands.

John snickered. "This is going to be so good. Where's Butch anyway? Why isn't she here hovering over you like a shadow?"

"I have no idea. I'm expecting her to show up any minute and drag me out like a cave man by my hair. She's not too keen on this whole thing."

"To be honest, I'd be a basket case if it were my hubby."

Faith grimaced. "Yeah, I know. I'm the worst wife in the world. Tell me and get it over with."

"You're not the worst wife. I'm just not into sharing and I have a distinct feeling that Reece feels the same way."

Suddenly, Alicia popped up. "Your big bad butch girlfriend having problems with this?"

Faith sneered. "She's my wife."

"Whatever. So, is she going to show up and try to scare me? I'm not afraid of her."

John laughed loudly. "Oh, Alicia, sweetheart, one mere look from Reece and you'd shit your little flowered panties."

"You think so?" Alicia asked with a grin.

John nodded. "I know so."

"I wear thongs." She looked Faith up and down. "I hope you smell better than you look right now, cuz I gotta be all up in your tits."

Faith growled. "Fuck off, Alicia."

Alicia chuckled and walked away.

John sucked his teeth. "She's just a bitch. You should bite her nipple really hard."

Faith laughed. "I think I just might."

†

Reece arrived at the set only to find a slew of security guards who weren't your garden variety rent-a-cops. They weren't wearing uniforms, in fact, if one didn't know better, no one would ever realize who these guys were. She circled the nondescript building a few times on her bike, eyeing all the entrances, and when the big guys left an opening for her to sneak in, she took advantage.

Not seeing what she'd like to see, Reece had an idea. Parking directly in front of the studio entrance, she got off her bike, tied down her helmet and pushed up her jacket sleeves, exposing her thick forearms. "Yo, Joe!" she yelled out, just knowing in all this burly manflesh, there had to be a Joe.

"What do you need Joe for?" the man at the entrance asked.

"I'm with the agency. Something's up and they need to talk to him right away. They sent me to cover."

The man looked Reece up and down. "Shit, I knew he'd fuck up." He nodded in Joe's direction.

Reece chuckled as she walked right through the unmanned door, shaking her head at the man's stupidity. She walked the halls confidently as if she belonged there, looking into every room searching for Faith. Reece's heart beat rapidly, hoping to find her, but afraid of what she'd find.

Finally stumbling upon the make-up room, she stepped in and looked around. Inside was the wardrobe room and there she found Faith's clothes. She picked up Faith's shirt and smelled it, inhaling deeply. Her heartbeat picked up speed and inhaled again before she got a pang deep in her chest.

"Oh, my God! Spike!"

Reece jerked the shirt from her face and glared angrily at the intruder.

John took one look into Reece's flashing eyes and crossed his legs.

"Where's Faith?"

"Outside, in the lot, in the back," John stuttered.

Reece dropped the shirt and growled. "Take me."

John squeezed his insides so he wouldn't pee in his pants. Reece was scaring him. He'd never seen that look in her eyes before. "I don't know… they're getting ready to shoot."

Reece seemed to expand to twice her size. "Do you really think I'll take no for an answer?"

The make-up artist blinked a few times. He was going to get in so much trouble, but he'd be damned if he told this woman no. He nodded, swallowed hard, grabbed the stuff he came for and walked out with Reece right behind him.

As John approached the film set, he turned once more to look at Reece. She was certainly on a mission and he didn't know if anyone could stop her. He loved Faith, and he had no idea what Reece was capable of doing, so he said a small prayer and gave it his best.

"Listen, right outside this door, is a live set. Faith is in this scene in a big way. Please, don't do anything stupid."

Reece sneered at him.

John tried again. "Please. For Faith."

Reece narrowed her eyes and gave a slight nod. He was right. She can't fuck this up for Faith. "I'm not here. Do you understand?"

John nodded and opened the door and suddenly it was nighttime, except for a small spot shining into a cop car. Reece squinted slightly, looking for her wife.

"All right! I need Meredith and Jesse here."

Reece followed the man's voice and saw Faith, dressed in a uniform, walking hesitantly toward the car. At first, seeing Faith dressed as a cop gave her a shiver—she hated cops. But when Faith turned around, and her shirt was all opened up, with a sexy bra peeking out, she hummed to herself. Until she saw Alicia. Then her hackles rose and her eyes narrowed.

John glanced at Reece, then back at the scene. Alicia strode confidently, a swagger to her step that made John grimace. She was such a bitch.

"All right. All right, you ready for a real woman?" Alicia asked cockily.

Faith rolled her eyes. "Just get in position."

Alicia leaned her back on the car, and Faith took her position in front of her.

"Okay, people, let's go."

Reece watched with her eyes wide as the man yelled action, and Faith threw herself onto Alicia. The two women began tearing at one another's clothes, mouths open, lips millimeters apart, breathing hard, and loud. Reece's stomach jolted and she thought she might throw up.

"I need you so much, baby."

"And I want you right now."

Alicia closed the gap between their mouths and they began kissing, passionately, hard. Alicia's tongue visibly invaded Faith's mouth, her hands grabbing at Faith's breasts.

John's heart pounded, almost as loud as Reece's.

Reece's fists clenched, her short nails dug into her palms. The loud groans and gasps echoed loudly in Reece's ears. Her eyes flashed dangerously as the two women tumbled into the back seat of the car, Faith on the bottom.

"Cut!"

Faith scrambled out from under Alicia, and grabbed her shirt closed. "John!"

John ran toward Faith, leaving Reece all alone.

†

Faith was fuming when John got to her, and he tried to calm her down. "What the hell happened? It looked fine from where we were!"

"That obnoxious bitch must have eaten a pound of freaking garlic! That little shit!" Faith spit on the floor. "Breathing all in my face, shoving her tongue in my mouth! God! *Ugh*! Tell me you have a mint!"

John glanced at Reece, who glared at him. "I'll get you one. Just let me fix the lipstick."

"Ooo, that…that…bitch! Look at her standing there laughing at me!"

Alicia smiled and winked, then laughed.

"I want to puke."

"Let's not and say we did. I'll give you a mint and before you know it, this will be all done."

"What's going on with you? Why aren't you commiserating with me and why are your hands shaking?"

John cleared his throat. "You hot lezzie mamas make me nervous," he joked.

Faith narrowed her eyes and studied her friend. "Well, okay, I'll buy that for now. Just hurry, my mouth tastes horrible!"

John dug around in his small bag and shoved two mints in Faith's mouth. She chewed them both and swished it all around in her mouth.

Reece wished she could hear what they were saying. She watched intently, rooted to the spot. She knew if she moved even an inch, she'd bolt to Faith's side and claim her as her own in front of all these people.

"All right, everyone back to their places. We'll take it from the back seat."

Reece's nostrils flared as John messed up Faith's hair and pulled open her shirt, just so. She watched, her eyes flashing a dangerous icy blue as Alicia climbed on top of her wife and whispered something that made Faith grimace.

The set went silent, the director yelled action, and Alicia tore open Faith's bra.

Reece growled, deep inside her chest. She'd had enough, she needed to leave. Now.

†

Faith was exhausted and couldn't think of anything except taking a hot shower and washing Alicia off her body. The ride home was quiet. Ted tried several times to strike up conversation to no avail. Faith was drained. She successfully shot almost all the love scenes needed. There were a few more, but those would come later. She was glad they were out of the way, but disgusted at the same time. Alicia did everything in her power to drive Faith insane. It took every ounce of strength for Faith to go beyond the here and now and put herself into character.

Alicia was no help by whispering horribly annoying things, her garlic breath, and the overuse of teeth when teeth weren't necessary. Still, Faith had to hand it to the woman for she really pulled it off. No matter how ugly Alicia thought being intimate with a woman was, she really made it believable. Faith wondered just what kind of skeletons Alicia had in her closet. After all, like it was said, *she who doth protest too much.*

Faith was proud of her performance too. As much as she detested Alicia, she was able to block it all out and go on with it. There were times when she wasn't looking at Alicia that she did pretend she was with Reece. Those times were pleasurable enough, even though Alicia didn't smell, feel or taste like Reece. If she pretended hard enough it worked. The actress sighed. She missed Reece terribly. After all the pretending, she needed to make love with Reece to ground herself. She hoped her wife was home, she needed to talk to her, to soothe her and to calm her down.

†

Faith stepped through the door with a relieved sigh. It was good to be home. Something was wrong though, Smudge didn't come to greet her. She turned on the lights to find Smudge in his pen. Curious, she dropped her bags down and called out for Reece. When there was no answer, she turned toward the kitchen for a drink. Suddenly, the lights went out and someone grabbed her from behind.

194

Faith screamed in fear, but stopped as soon as she realized they were her lover's arms. Reece's mouth roughly covered hers in a kiss that was almost brutal and she could hardly breathe. The momentum of Reece's body weight shoved Faith into the wall and she hit it quite hard. "Mmm!" she grunted, trying to push Reece off. "Mmm!"

Reece, her chest heaving rapidly, backed off. The ray of a streetlight fell across her face and Faith shivered at the look in those eyes. She swallowed hard as the sound of their breathing filled the room. She licked her lips. "Reece?" she asked tentatively.

The Animal growled and wrapped her hand around Faith's wrist bringing the hand to her face. "Is this the hand you fucked her with?" She smelled it. "Is it?"

Faith closed her eyes to lose eye contact. Fear, excitement, anticipation, and lust zinged through her body like sparks. "Reece, I didn't…"

"I saw you. I was there." A large hand covered Faith's sex roughly. "Whose pussy is this?"

Faith's nostrils flared. Reece was there—she saw it. She was staking her claim. "Yours, only yours." She could already feel herself getting wet.

Blue eyes narrowed and Reece tightened her grip. "Mine."

Faith nodded, her heart beating hard and fast. The Animal. It had been so long and she was very eager to welcome her. She stared defiantly into pale blue eyes, her heart pounding with excitement. She licked her lips.

The Animal's nostrils flared and she crushed Faith's lips in a searing, bruising kiss. She could feel Faith's resistance and it fed her desire to control. Without warning, she ripped her lips away and threw Faith over her shoulder, took her to the other room and dropped her on the couch. She stood above the actress, chest rising and falling rapidly, her jaw clenched.

Faith's eyes sparkled with want, lying there, with the Animal's eyes devouring her. There was a long forgotten fire coursing through her veins. She wanted this, needed this, to connect with Reece on a primal level. She bowed her head slightly, and looked up at Reece coyly.

Reece slammed her hands on the couch, landing them on either side of Faith's head. "I don't appreciate you baring those tits, my tits, for anyone, let alone an audience, Faith."

Reece's breath was hot and smelled of liquor, her voice was a deep purr, threatening, yet extremely arousing and Faith felt a surge of want rise from her gut. "They're yours."

"Then why are you sticking them in that slut's mouth? If they're mine, they belong in my mouth." Reece slid one hand from the couch, down Faith's shoulder, hooking her fingers in the neck of Faith's shirt. "I don't want to share them." With a swift tug, the material tore, exposing Faith's breasts. Reece's mouth watered and she licked her lips. "Put them in my mouth."

The Animal's icy blue gaze never wavered. Faith's heart thrummed as she lifted up and arched her back, her left nipple making contact with glistening lips. Reece inhaled deeply, consuming Faith's scent.

"I could swallow you whole, Faith."

Faith shivered as the hot breath fell across her nipple. "Then do it."

The Animal lunged forward, opening her mouth wide and devouring. She sucked the flesh deeply, hungrily, growling loudly in her chest.

Faith arched her back as far as she could, trying to force more of her breast into Reece's mouth.

Reece dragged her teeth across Faith's tit, until they closed on her nipple. She bit down.

Faith yelled out in surprise and pain.

Reece chuckled. "You want me to hurt you?" she asked through her teeth.

Faith swallowed hard. It was true. She wanted The Animal to hurt her. She squeezed her eyes shut against the delicious pain and sharp teeth bit into her flesh. She waited holding her breath for Reece to grasp the ring. She knew that was next. Hoped it was next.

"You like it."

Faith groaned a high-pitched wanting sound. She did want it. She felt she deserved it as punishment for doing the sex scene. "Harder."

The Animal moaned loudly and grabbed Faith's head with both hands, engulfing it. She demanded a kiss and took the waiting mouth with force, plunging her tongue inside, claiming it.

Faith wanted this.

The semi-consciousness of Reece, lurking beneath the surface, was able to let go and take what she wanted. She threw herself onto Faith, pulling her face impossibly close.

The weight of her lover was just what she needed. Surrounded by and encompassed by Reece, she desperately needed connecting and threw her legs around the larger woman. She opened her mouth wide. The kiss was ravaging and their teeth clashed while their tongues battled roughly.

Reece emitted an animalistic sound and twisted their entwined bodies so that Faith's back was flat on the couch. She released her head with one hand and used that hand to snake between them and rip off the rest of the blond's shirt. Faith's legs squeezed her strongly as The Animal pawed her breasts.

Faith tore her mouth away to gasp for breath.

Reece narrowed her dilated eyes. "Let go of me and take off those pants. Now."

Faith struggled to remove them as her wife lifted up a few inches. She could smell the alcohol on her breath, mixed with the musky smell of Reece's sweat. The combination turned her on, even more than she thought possible.

"Hurry up, Faith, I want to see my pussy."

The actress finished quickly, her panties in a ball on the floor. She finally caught her breath, when Reece palmed her wet sex. "God! I can smell how hot you are for me. How much you want me to fuck you."

Faith gasped loudly as Reece suddenly plunged two fingers into her depths.

"So fucking hot and wet."

Reece's voice was harsh, and raspy, betraying her own arousal and Faith ate it up. She knew when Reece was like this, she didn't want Faith to talk much unless she asked her to, but with her long fingers immobile, she needed to speak. "Fuck me, please. Do it."

The Animal chuckled a dangerous chuckle. "Oh, no. You fuck me. Show me how horny this pussy is for me."

Faith adjusted herself and thrust down, impaling herself with a loud moan.

Reece put her lips onto Faith's ear. "That's it... you're my hot horny bitch. Do you understand that? Only mine."

Faith nodded, never missing a thrust, desperately filling herself with her lover's fingers. She grabbed Reece's shoulders and dug in with her fingers, using the strong woman's body for leverage.

Wild blue eyes watched intently as Faith engulfed her fingers. Her own sex on fire from the display, The Animal groaned painfully. "That's my girl. You need me."

"Yes!" Faith agreed emphatically. "Need you," she gasped.

Reece leaned a knee on the couch to free up her other hand. She covered Faith's mouth with her own as she began to rub her clit, swallowing her loud scream. Faith's inner walls clenched at her fingers, and she began to thrust faster, erratically. "Look at me when you come," she demanded in a deep purr.

Faith fixed her gaze on The Animal's half lidded, lust filled eyes. "Yes...God—"

Reece's teeth shone in the darkness as Faith's muscles contracted sharply around her fingers. The smaller woman shuddered, and groaned, her nails digging deeply into Reece's shoulders. Her green eyes focused, unwavering, on her own, sharing the depth of the moment with only her.

"Ohhhh...Reece!"

The Animal let out the breath she was holding as Faith began to relax. She felt her own clit twitching, begging for release, but for some reason, instead of demanding pleasure, she dropped herself back down on top of Faith.

"Beautiful," she mumbled, burying her face in Faith's slick neck.

"I love you, Reece. Only you."

The Animal shivered as Reece came into her own skin. "Thank you for that."

Faith moaned and twitched as Reece withdrew her fingers. "I needed you so badly."

Reece hummed. "Me, too.

When Faith woke early in the morning, Reece wasn't in bed. She stretched and smiled to herself. She loved her wife. Plain and simple. They had wound up ravaging one another for most of the evening in the living room, the kitchen, and even the shower, like they were starved. Faith turned and smelled Reece's pillow. Where was she anyway? Not really wanting to get out of bed, but curious as to why Reece would be up so early, she tossed the blanket off reluctantly and went searching.

Chapter Fifteen

Reece was up at the crack of dawn, and even though she had expended an enormous amount of energy the previous evening, she felt rejuvenated. With Smudge laying on her face most of the night; she was the first to know how much he needed a bath. She stroked him lightly until he woke up. After he yawned and stretched, Reece took him down for water and breakfast, and then took him for a walk.

It was during that odd hour of morning. The streets of New York were virtually empty and it was almost eerie as they walked. Reece looked over her shoulder every inch of the way.

Faith heard Reece's low voice coming from the bathroom and was thoroughly puzzled at who she could be talking to in there. She opened the door slowly, and found her big muscular wife holding the small dog in one hand, three fingers of the other hand working shampoo into Smudge's coat. She was speaking to him the whole time with little words of praise, and kissed him square on the nose several times. Faith left the bathroom silently and smiled. She'd have to ask Reece why she felt the need to wash the dog at such an early hour, but for now, they looked so sweet, she couldn't interrupt the moment.

Reece rinsed her dog off and wrapped him in an enormous towel. "Now you smell like the handsome man I love," she cooed and started to rub the tiny dog dry. She paid special attention to his tail and ears, softly telling him what a good boy he was being. Now came the hard part, the evil blow dryer. Not wanting to wake Faith with the noise, she took the dryer, wrapped up Smudge and headed downstairs. Reece was surprised to see Faith wrapped up in her robe, sitting on the couch drinking coffee.

"Oh, you're up already? I didn't wake you, did I?"

Faith snickered at the giant wad of towel with a teensy nose poking out of it. "No, baby. Why are you washing him?"

Reece sat the bundle down on the couch and plugged in the dryer. "He has a follow up at the vet with his ear. I didn't want them to think he smells."

Faith laughed. "You don't bathe me when I have a doctor's appointment."

Reece waggled her eyebrows. "You'd never make it to the doctor."

The actress grinned. She could never resist that sexy look Reece was giving her and she jumped up to kiss her wife.

Reece looked hesitant. "Look, about last night, I…"

Faith smiled reassuringly. "I wanted it. I needed it."

"I just don't want to be too rough for you."

"Baby, you would never hurt me and if I'd said no, I'm sure even the Animal would stop. I trust you." She wrapped her arms around Reece and kissed her shoulder. "I felt like I was losing you, and I wanted you back. I miss you, Reece."

"I miss you too, Faith. Let's not do that again." Reece pulled her wife closer.

They stood basking in one another's embrace until Smudge whined.

"Reece, he can't move." Faith giggled.

"I didn't want him catching a cold." Reece shrugged. "I better dry him. We have to leave soon."

Faith pouted. "I don't want to let go of you."

"And I don't really want you to."

Faith turned in Reece's arms so her back pressed against her wife and she rested her arms on Reece's, softly stroking her hands. "Is it a bad thing to want to be in your arms all day?"

Blue eyes fluttered shut from the sensation. Reece kissed the top of Faith's head and sighed. "Not at all. I'd like that too."

"I have an early day. Do you have to go to work tonight?"

Reece shivered a little as Faith's nails trailed up and down her arms. "Nope, but I have clients at the gym. I should be done by three."

Faith smiled. "Well, you just shower and get comfortable after that and wait for me."

Reece raised an eyebrow. "What do you have planned?"

"Just sitting in your arms."

"Mmm. I like that plan."

Reluctantly they parted and Faith went up to change for work.

"Where will you be today?" Reece called up after her.

"Brooklyn, the address is on a paper by the phone."

Reece looked at the address and nodded, scooping up the bundle of towel and dog. "Come on, little man, it's dryer time."

†

Faith heard the blow dryer and in seconds Smudge screamed. She ran to see what happened and stopped halfway down the stairs. Reece had the dog against her chest, the blower at arm's length, facing them both. One finger and a thumb from the hand Reece was holding the dog with, was covering his ears and his nose was stuck under her arm. She was kissing Smudge's head and constantly moving the blower as the dog shook in fear.

Faith smiled warmly and sat on the step to watch. The same woman who had ravaged her the night before, who beat people for walking on the same side of the street as her, was as gentle and soft as she was brutal. Faith shook her head at the enigma that was Reece, then felt tears coming on.

Sometimes she felt her heart would explode from the love she felt for this woman. Reece was hard, as hard as any puzzle Faith tried to solve, but she loved her with all her heart and soul.

When Reece completed her task, she put the small dog down on the coffee table and examined his ears. "Looks good from where I am, little man. Let that mean old doctor find a speck of dirt in there. I dare him."

Faith cleared her throat as she approached her lover, and smiled when Reece turned in her direction and grinned.

"I have to take him to the vet now. Will you be here when we get back?"

Faith shook her head. "No, I have to leave soon, too."

Reece stood. "Then come here so I can kiss you."

Faith needed no further instruction and walked right into Reece's very warm body. "God, you're so hot!"

"Yeah, it's the blow dryer. I had to hit me with it, too."

Faith grinned. "You spoil that dog silly." She leaned in for a kiss and got one.

Reece inhaled Faith's perfume and hummed. "You smell so good I could eat you up."

The actress laughed. "Save that thought for later, tiger."

Reece watched her wife walk back up the stairs and sighed. "Ya know, little man, she looks just as good going as she does coming."

†

Reece decided that since Smudge just had a bath, he needed a shirt and she dressed him for the walk to the vet. "I'm going," she called out.

Faith came down to say good-bye and shook her head.

"What?" Reece wondered.

"I told you that collar is too big for him and where did he get that shirt?"

Reece looked down at the dog. "I got it for him. It's a licensed Harley shirt and he likes it."

Faith knelt down and picked up the dog. "Well, I guess your Mommy has no say in your choice of clothing anymore." She kissed the dog. "Honestly, Reece." She smoothed out Smudge's shirt. "A naked woman on a bike?"

Reece took the dog away from Faith. "He's a biker dog."

Faith chuckled. "Okay, you go take Goliath. Don't forget, I want you home tonight."

Reece narrowed her eyes. Faith definitely had more plans than just laying around. She grinned. "I'll be here."

Chapter Sixteen

"Goliath, you're next."

Reece walked into the exam room and smugly stood the dog on the table. "Go on, check those ears," she dared the vet.

The doctor looked at the shirt and grinned, then took out a long cotton swab. Reece felt queasy as he stuck it into Smudge's tiny ear. However, she leaned forward, her head almost touching the vet's as he pulled it out and they both examined it. "See? Clean." She folded her arms across her chest.

"You did a great job, Ms. Corbett. However." He lifted a little paw. "His nails need a trim."

Reece frowned. She thought she had trimmed them, but with all the chaos in her life lately she must have forgot. "Oh," she said quietly. "I'll do it when I get home."

"Nonsense, he's here. I'll do it."

Reece narrowed her eyes as he picked up a huge guillotine looking nail clipper. He clipped several nails without amputating anything so she relaxed. Just as she felt comfortable, Smudge screamed. She grabbed him off the table and picked up his leg. "He's bleeding! You cut off his toe!" She panicked.

The doctor snickered. "It's nothing, I just snipped too low." He took some yellow powder and tried to put it on the dog's nail but Reece wouldn't give him the paw. "Ms. Corbett, this will stop the bleeding, if you just let me—"

"What is that? Will it hurt? I bet it'll burn! Nonsense you said, he's here, you'll do it! He's hemorrhaging!"

"Ms. Corbett! Please!" A small tug of war took place. A technician entered the room after hearing the raised voices and eased the dog from Reece. "It's fine, this happens all the time."

Reece scowled at the young woman. "Not when I do it."

After the doctor held the styptic powder on the nail, it stopped bleeding. "You'll want to keep this dry for a few hours."

Reece glared at him. He picked up the nail clipper again and Reece quickly took her dog. "No, thank you, I'll finish it myself."

She muttered foul things all the way through the office and slammed the door behind her. "Of all the stupid fucking things." She pulled the small dog up to her face and scrutinized the nail. It wasn't bleeding anymore, but Smudge was trembling. "I got you, little man, you just relax."

†

Faith walked into the makeshift make-up trailer and stopped dead in her tracks. "What's she doing here?" She pointed to Alicia who was sitting in the chair.

John looked up with a disgusted expression. "Her girl is out sick, so I have to take care of her."

Faith glared at him, Alicia smiled condescendingly, and John rolled his eyes.

"So, Faith, you looked pretty flustered when you left yesterday. Was it something I did?" Alicia chuckled.

Faith narrowed her eyes. "Alicia, you could be naked and covered in honey and you still couldn't turn me on."

Alicia laughed as Faith approached the chair to kiss John hello. She noticed Faith's large hickey. "Holy shit, your dyke did that?" She pointed to the spot.

Faith sighed and regretted ever coming close to her. "My wife did a lot more than that. Jealous?"

Alicia sucked her teeth. "Don't be an ass. I need dick. I don't care about what your wife does to you."

"You should. They may start thinking you did it in the heat of a moment. Besides, who says I don't get dick, too."

John, used to the snarking between the two women, just snickered and studied the mark. "Ooo, a good time was had by all I see?"

Faith grinned devilishly. "A very good time." She and John giggled together.

"Don't make me puke." Alicia sneered.

"I'll be back when she's gone," Faith announced as she left, winking at John.

"What does she mean she gets dick, too?"

John studied Alicia before answering. She was seriously asking and he wondered if he should answer her. "Haven't you ever heard of a strap-on?"

Alicia looked thoughtful and John hurried to finish her hair.

†

Reece found that if she actually paid attention to the muscles she was training, instead of the bodies they belonged to, that working with the women wasn't so difficult. Of course, this didn't happen right away. The first two clients were sexy, lithe young women, half-dressed, and eager to touch her. It was torture for Reece and she stripped off her t-shirt only to reveal scratch marks and other battle scars from the previous night. This led to very curious stares and other personal questions. Finally able to leave, Reece practically ran out the door.

†

Faith actually liked her police uniform. Even though it was just a costume, she felt somewhat powerful, carrying the gun belt and nightstick. The handcuffs brought back some pretty good memories, too. She toyed with the thought of sneaking the uniform home to have some fun with Reece, and then thought better of it. She wasn't too sure Reece could get accustomed to anyone, even her, in a police uniform.

It was a good day. A lot got accomplished, except for one strange incident. Since it was an independent film, low on budget, they didn't always get the right permits to film on the streets of Brooklyn. At times, they ran to a location, shot scenes quickly, disappearing before anyone could notice.

Unfortunately, as she and Alicia were chasing a perp, the real police joined in, assuming two of their own needed help. Imagine everyone's surprise when they caught the guy and two other real officers ran to cuff him. It was a lot of fast-talking, embarrassment, and convincing, and in the end, a fine was issued.

Faith grinned, thinking about it now, as she stripped off the uniform to go home. She had some plans with her sexy wife, and was very eager to get there.

†

Reece couldn't wait to strip off her gym clothes and did so as soon as she got home. Leaving a trail of dirty clothes wasn't her usual behavior, as she knew Faith hated that, but she figured she'd be finished with her shower before Faith came home.

That wasn't the case. As soon as Reece turned on the water, Faith walked in. She was about to call out for her lover, but saw the clothes strewn around. She grinned, and picked up the tank top, smelling it. Before Reece, sweat was gross, but Reece's sweat turned her on. She found that out when they made love. Reece sweated a lot and she loved the feeling of her slick body and the taste of her salty skin. Faith closed her eyes as a wave of arousal washed across her. She turned her gaze to the top of the stairs and smiled seductively. The shower was running, her naked wife was in there, soapy and wet. She dropped the shirt and headed up the stairs.

†

Reece was in the middle of washing her hair when she sensed Faith. Grinning, she turned to face the spray, allowing Faith to sneak into the shower with her. A few seconds later, another set of hands slid into her soapy hair. Softly, Faith massaged her scalp, sliding her hands through the slippery strands.

"Mmm, feels good," Reece purred.

Faith slipped her hands down Reece's neck and across her shoulders. She continued down her arms, and finally, slid them around her waist, pressing herself into Reece's back.

"Hi, baby," Faith murmured into the wet skin.

"Hi, yourself. Is this part of your plan?" Reece turned around in the embrace and tilted her head back, allowing the water to wash across her.

Faith was mesmerized, wishing she could turn herself into water and cascade over every inch of Reece's glorious body at once. She stepped back and away from her lover, drinking in the sight before her. "God, you're so, so…God."

Reece, unable to hear above the water crashing on her head, just stood there, unaware of what she was doing to Faith.

Faith placed her hands on Reece's abdomen, and spread her fingers, trying to touch as much skin as possible, pressing into the hard flesh, savoring the feel of the hard muscle rippling under the soft skin.

Feeling the touch, Reece stepped forward, and watched Faith as she stared openly at her naked body. She loved how Faith looked at her, studied her, and devoured her with her eyes. She loved the myriad of expressions that crossed her face. Wonder, passion, need, hunger.

Faith looked up to find Reece watching her, clear blue eyes staring right into hers. She tilted her head back, and parted her lips in an invitation. Reece accepted and lowered her head in a tender, loving kiss.

They washed one another, slowly, sensually, hardly speaking at all, just instinctively knowing what the other was thinking, and needing. After they dried one another, Faith led Reece to the bed, and instructed her to lie down on her stomach. Faith straddled her lover's thighs and began to map out her body with her fingertips. She started at the strong prominent shoulders, caressing them, touching them, grasping them, then moved down the back. She slid her hands across the large expanse of strong muscle, sometimes using her nails, sometimes just the tips of her fingers, drawing sensuous sighs and the occasional twitch from Reece.

"You're killing me, Faith," Reece whispered.

"Shh. Indulge me."

Blue eyes fluttered closed as Faith dragged her nails gently down Reece's back, teasing her sensitive sides, meeting again in the middle. Faith watched closely, as the muscles reacted to her touch. Gooseflesh sprouted on her lover's skin and Reece squirmed, writhing gently, not fighting when Faith hit a sensitive spot. Her heart leapt as Reece lay there, completely at her mercy, full of trust, allowing her control. Faith adjusted her position, to kneel over Reece's calves and brought her hungry hands to the most perfect buttocks she had ever laid eyes on. She squeezed them with both hands, even dug her nails in a little, and grinned a bit cockily knowing no one but her had ever done this before. Only her. She licked her lips and leaned forward, dropping kisses across Reece's back, her eyes closing as Reece arched into the touch.

"I love you so much. Sometimes, I can't believe how lucky I am that you love me."

Reece's eyes opened and she blinked several times. "What?"

Faith ran her fingers indulgently through Reece's wet hair. "There are days I marvel at how lucky I am to have you in my life."

Reece turned beneath Faith and sat up. She stared in disbelief. "Faith, I am the one who's lucky."

Faith took Reece's hands in her own. "Oh, Reece…"

Reece brought their hands up so she could cup Faith's face. "No, don't you understand? I was nothing before I met you. I had nothing and I was nothing. You saved my life. You made me something."

Faith sobbed and threw herself at Reece. "God, I love you."

"Are you crying?" Reece wrapped her arms around Faith and held her tightly, concerned.

"Sometimes, you just say these things, and my heart feels like it may explode from loving you."

Reece kissed the top of Faith's head and closed her eyes, enjoying the feel of Faith loving her. Without agendas, without questions, she loved her. And she was not afraid. Reece sighed, with contentment and a sudden feeling of release.

Faith began leaving small kisses on Reece's shoulder. At first, in adoration, but suddenly aware of their naked bodies touching, her tongue snaked out and it became a little more than kissing.

Reece inhaled quickly as sharp teeth pulled the skin on her neck. She leaned back on her elbows, giving Faith an invitation.

Faith sat back on her heels, looking into trusting, wanting blue eyes and swallowed hard. Her gaze swept across Reece's body and she had to catch her breath. This, all of this was hers and she was going to thank Reece for the gift.

Reece tried to watch Faith love her, but when warm lips closed around her nipple, her head fell back. A skilled tongue worked around her hard flesh, and she groaned when Faith nipped at it with her teeth. Reece's back arched slightly as Faith began teasing her other nipple with her fingers, circling it, brushing her fingertips against it, driving her crazy. Her entire body was hyper sensitive to Faith's touch, and it felt like heaven.

Faith hummed in pleasure as Reece tried to force her breast into her hand. Instead, she trailed her hot tongue across Reece's chest and around the neglected nipple. Reece groaned louder, leaning on one elbow as she tried to push Faith's head down closer.

"Don't tease, Faith," Reece said in a raspy voice.

Faith chuckled lightly. "Patience."

Reece shivered as Faith's hot breath fell on her wet flesh. "But I want you," she groaned.

Reece's deep groans were always her downfall and Faith began to trail her tongue along the underside of her lover's breasts. Reece wound her strong fingers through Faith's hair, pulling her closer, silently begging for more.

Faith began her journey downward, slowly, torturously licking and tasting everything under her touch. Reece's ribs, the vee where her ribcage met, the indentation down the middle of her prominent abs—abs that were almost undulating under her tongue. She stopped to kiss Reece's navel, swirling her tongue around it in an imitation of what was to come.

Reece growled in her throat, squeezing her fingers around her wife's head, her sex throbbing for attention. "Please, Faith…" she breathed, moaning as Faith's tongue left a hot trail across her stomach. She jerked her hips, seeking relief.

Faith inhaled deeply, Reece's strong scent produced a shudder, knowing how wet her lover was for her. "I can't wait to taste you," she murmured into Reece's lower belly, nipping the sensitive skin with her teeth. Reece jumped and grunted in frustration, yet remained submissive. Faith's nostrils flared as the scent of her wife's arousal became stronger, and she ventured lower, Reece's fingers digging painfully hard into her scalp.

"Sweet Jesus!" Reece blurted as Faith's tongue speared through her wetness. "Fuck." Her knees came up and squeezed Faith's head, then fell open as her wife flattened her tongue and licked slowly.

"Ummm." Faith hummed in pleasure at the taste and feel of Reece under her tongue. She brought her hands up and rested them on Reece's tight stomach, to lavish in the feel of the muscles playing under her fingers. She opened her eyes, taking in the sight of her strong dangerous lover, defenseless under her touch. Reece arched and moaned wordlessly and Faith's eyes rolled shut in her own ecstasy.

She rolled her tongue around in the abundant wetness she invoked and groaned. Reece bucked, nearly throwing her when she swiped her tongue across her clit. Her lover's long fingers lost their grip in her hair and searched out her shoulders. Faith looked up again at her magnificent wife, her long neck stretched back, her mouth open, breathing out sounds of pleasure. Faith's sex clenched at the sight of Reece's muscular arms, stretched taut, gripping her shoulders tight.

"Please, Faith...Please..."

Faith growled and sucked Reece's clit between her lips. Her lover practically left the bed with a loud moan of relief. Faith suckled it rhythmically, never closing her eyes, taking in the work of art that was Reece reaching orgasm. Reece's jaw clenched, her knees closed around Faith's head, her fingers spasmed in time with her stomach and with a loud drawn out string of muttered nonsense, Reece succumbed. Her back arched off the bed, her hips thrust into Faith's face, and for a split second, when their eyes met, Faith swore she caught a glimpse of Reece's soul.

Reece twitched as they lay there, arms entwined with legs, catching their breath. Faith only moved when Reece released a long sated sigh, and her legs fell to the bed. She rested her head on Reece's thigh and stroked her stomach until she relaxed.

"God, come up here. I want to hold you."

Faith climbed up and arms engulfed her in a tight hug. "I adore you, Reece."

"I don't know what I did to deserve you," Reece breathed into Faith's hair.

Faith knew there was no sense in answering. She just lay there, contented, wrapped in the comfort of her wife's arms.

Chapter Seventeen

Faith awoke some time later with a smile on her lips. She peeked open an eye to watch Reece draw idle circles around her nipple, and remained silent until Reece began to play with the ring. "What are you doing?" Faith asked, turning on her side to face her lover.

"We should get you something sexier than just this plain ring," Reece replied, never taking her gaze, or her fingers, from Faith's breast.

Faith looked down and watched her nipple tighten and pucker. "Like what?"

"Like maybe a barbell." She stuck out her tongue to display her barbell.

"That's too big," Faith said with a teasing wink.

Reece grinned. "You know what I mean." She leaned and placed a light kiss on the nipple in question.

"Mmm, don't start something now, I'm starving."

Reece rolled and looked at the clock on the nightstand. "It's past dinner. No wonder you're hungry." She turned onto her back, arms behind her head.

Faith rolled and threw her leg over Reece's, and settled her head on her wife's shoulder. "I don't want to move. Can't we just blink our eyes, or wiggle our nose and make food appear?"

Reece chuckled, and brought an arm down to surround Faith. "If I had magic powers, I wouldn't be using them for food."

Faith slapped her lover lightly. "That's because you're a pig. I don't even want to know what you're thinking."

"I think I showed you every thought," Reece said with a leer. Her stomach growled loudly and she looked down at it. "I guess we'd better get something to eat."

Faith agreed. "Mm, hmm."

Neither woman moved.

The phone rang and Reece reached to get it. "Yeah?"

She heard a lot of loud noise and music. "Are you all right?"

Reece was annoyed. "Yeah, Cor, I'm fine."

"She's just concerned," Faith whispered, stroking Reece's arm.

"Oh, soooo, everything is okay?" Cori asked, wishing Faith had answered the phone.

Reece handed the phone to Faith. "Here, you talk. She wants details. I'll get food."

Faith took the phone and laughed. "I kept her home tonight, is everything all right there without her?"

"Yeah, it's fine, just worried about you two."

"Well, worry no more, we're okay now." Faith replied, sitting up in bed.

"You sure? Cuz I didn't like what was happening."

"Positive." Faith said dreamily. "Cori, I am so deeply, totally in love with that impossible woman."

"You know the feeling is entirely mutual."

"Yeah, I do." She smiled remembering Reece's confession.

"No, I mean it, seriously. I've known her a long time, and well, she's changed totally."

"She told me as much this afternoon and I was floored. I guess I just took for granted the effect I've had on her."

Cori's eyes widened. "She told you? You didn't have to torture her or anything? She just told you?"

Faith smiled. "Yep. It was one of the most beautiful moments I've had in my life."

"What was?" Reece asked holding a bottle of water out.

Faith accepted the water. "Nothing, baby. Cor, I gotta go, I'm starved."

Cori snickered. "I see we worked up an appetite?"

"And then some," Faith responded with a purr.

"Sluts," Cori teased. "Take care of her, I'll hold down the fort."

†

Sometime in the middle of the night, Reece became restless. Having slept half the afternoon and most of the night had her awake and antsy. Bored with the TV and not wanting to wake Faith, she put on jeans and a t-shirt, kissed Smudge on the head, and went to the club. It wasn't that she didn't trust Cori, Sarge, or the rest of the staff, she just needed the familiarity of the routine.

She rolled her bike down the block and around the corner so she wouldn't wake Faith. Faith knew the sound of Reece's bike even in a dead sleep. She idled at a red light and looked around at the people on the street. The populace was made up of late night stragglers, probably leaving bars but many maybe working the night shift or just getting out. There were some homeless scattered around, as well. It was a nice night and if she looked hard enough, she could see a few stars. The light changed and she drove off, thinking about the people she'd seen, wondering if they felt how she felt, or if she was the only one. How did she feel? She couldn't put words to it, but something had changed. She felt different, lighter, less edgy and frustrated.

It wasn't just a feeling either, it was a sense, like touch and hearing, and she didn't mean a sixth sense like extrasensory perception. She felt a new level of awareness. Like tonight for instance. The air seemed sweeter, even in New York City. And when Faith was touching her, merely running her fingers across her back, she'd felt more alive than she had in her whole life. It was like all her senses were on overdrive. She swore she could even taste Faith by just touching her. It confused her, the idea of not being able to name it, but it was a good feeling. All the feelings were good, so she didn't make herself crazy trying to name it.

Pulling up to the club, she uncharacteristically parked on the street, and tucked her helmet under her arm. There were a few people on the street around the entrance, and just as she opened the door, a photographer in a parked car started taking pictures of her. She turned and growled. She knew better than to flatten him so she sneered angrily and gave him the finger with both hands.

"Fuck off," she growled, running at him, grabbing his lens and bringing the camera down. "I'll destroy the fucking thing and then start on you." She stared him down for some time, apparently frightening him sufficiently enough to roll up his darkly tinted window.

"Can't have a goddamned moment's peace anymore," she muttered, storming into the club.

As soon as the throbbing music and din of the crowd hit her, she felt more at ease. She was safe in her club, in familiar territory. She walked through the crowd, and looked around. One table held a group of businessmen, making deals, their papers strewn across the table. She saw a group of jocks with a dancer, probably blowing their allowance in tips, and across the stage was a woman getting an eyeful of one of the dancers. Finally spotting Cori's ridiculous hair, she made her way in that direction. As she neared, she saw Cori talking with two men, and could see by the dancer's expression she was near tears with boredom. Reece grinned devilishly, snuck up behind her, and pinched her ass hard. She got a quick slap in the face for her prank and stared agape at Cori.

"Oh, my God! Reece! I had no idea... I'm so sorry," Cori babbled.

Reece closed her mouth and chuckled, rubbing her sore cheek. "Jeez, Cor, I don't have to worry about you at all," she half-joked.

"Reece, really, I'm sorry. You wanna hit me back?" Cori was horrified.

Reece shook her head and smiled. "Nah, I guess I shouldn't have snuck up on you. But consider yourself warned. Next time you slap me, I will throw you over my knee and spank the shit out of you."

"Only if Vi can watch," Cori replied eagerly.

"Freak."

"You love me for my freakitude."

Reece rolled her eyes and chuckled.

†

Reece was studying the books in her office when a knock sounded. She ignored it, knowing it could only be Cori. Sure enough, there was another knock, followed by the doorknob moving. Reece stood and unlocked the door and Cori practically fell into the room.

"You're a dick, Reece," she complained.

Reece laughed. "Awww, are you embarrassed?"

"Fuck off." Cori flopped into Reece's desk chair. "Hey, so what happened with Faith? I have it on good authority you guys humped like horny teenagers."

"Get up, freak." Reece picked Cory up and dropped her onto the couch. Then she sat in her chair. "Is that what Faith said?"

"No, but I have a hunch."

"Horny teenagers, huh?" Reece grinned. "Not really. Maybe yesterday…"

Cori watched the play of emotions on Reece's face and cocked her head. "Twenty for your thoughts."

Reece's eyebrow shot up.

"Hey, inflation."

"Don't really know if I can tell you," Reece said with a pensive look.

"Come on, you know you can always talk to me."

"I don't know if I can explain it."

Cory studied her friend. "Try."

Reece propped her feet up on the desk and leaned back. "You know how I used to be, right? Well, that's gone. I don't even remember how it used to feel to be me. Even the Animal is different. I don't know—"

"How so?"

Reece furrowed her brows and picked at a fingernail. "I can't explain it that well but yesterday, when I thought I was gone for sure, I wasn't. The Animal comes and usually I disappear, but I was there, all of me, at the same time, and it was like I felt everything twice. And tonight, I still felt everything twice, every touch, and every breath was like… so much more than one." Reece scrunched her face up. "I don't think I can explain it."

"Wow." Cori stared at Reece. "That is so fucking awesome."

Reece looked intensely at Cori. "Faith did that. I don't know how and I don't know why."

They fell silent, and even though they were both thinking the same thing—*thank God for Faith*—neither one spoke.

†

Faith was relaxing in the tub, a cup of coffee at her side. She had also brought the phone with her in case Reece called. She wasn't disappointed to find Reece gone that morning, she knew that too much laying around made her crazy.

Soon enough, the phone did ring and when she answered it, it wasn't who she expected.

"Faith?"

"Daddy?"

"Hello."

Faith swallowed hard. "How are you?"

"Fine," Mr. Ashford replied quickly.

Faith gave him a chance. She was surprised that he called so soon after the news, and wanted him to speak first.

"About this movie thing," he started, hesitantly.

"Yes?"

228

"Look," he sighed heavily. "I guess it's all right. I mean, I can't stop you from doing it and after some thought, I realize you're not doing it just to make me and your mother crazy. I won't watch it, Faith."

"I understand, Dad. Thank you." Faith closed her eyes and breathed a sigh of relief.

"I don't like it either. Not one stinking bit. I just want you to know that."

"Daddy, I know the guys talk and I'm sorry they do. I'm sorry it hurts you."

"Faith, you're my daughter and though I make mistakes, I always love you."

"Thank you. I love you, too."

"Your mother wants to talk to you."

Faith heard the commotion of the phone passing between them and shook her head with a smile.

"Dear?"

"Yeah, Ma."

"Is everything… settled between you two?"

Faith grinned. "Yes, it is."

"Good. Theresa was so miserable."

Faith blinked. *Reece was miserable? What about me?* "It's all taken care of. Reece is fine now."

"Thank heavens. And you?"

"Gee, thanks, I'm the afterthought."

"Faith, now you know that's not true."

"I'm fine too. We're both good."

"Well, then, now that that's done, I can go back to my show."

Faith chuckled. "I love you too, Ma."

†

Reece stood, staring wide-eyed at the naked woman in front of her. "What part of I'm married don't you understand?"

"So, she'll never know. I won't tell."

Reece shook her head. "Put some clothes on, you're embarrassing yourself." She turned to walk away and jumped as her ass was caressed. "Excuse me?"

Naked girl smiled seductively. "Come on, sexy. I've always had this fantasy of you taking me hard and fast with your strong arms pinning me to the wall." She closed in on Reece.

Reece's adrenaline rushed. There was a time she wouldn't have thought twice. Shoulders straight, she walked out of the locker room.

†

Faith broke the lip-lock with Alicia as the director yelled *cut*. She wiped her mouth and rolled her eyes at the annoying smirk on Alicia's face. "Why do you make this so difficult?"

Alicia chuckled. "Because it's fun to annoy you. Besides, I thought that was an appropriate thing to do."

Faith rolled her tongue around in her mouth. "Biting my tongue was appropriate? Ugh."

John approached the two sniping women. "Okay, 'nuff of that. Faith, let's go fix that neck."

As John reapplied cover up to Faith's hickeys, Alicia stepped into the van.

"What do you want, Nancy?"

Faith laughed. "Nancy?"

"Yeah, I had a psychotic cousin Nancy. I thought it fit."

"Very funny, Mary," Alicia shot back.

"Oh, I'm devastated. No one's ever called me Mary before." John feigned pain.

Alicia stewed.

Just then, there was a knock on the side of the van. "Come!" John yelled.

The door opened, and Reece walked in.

"Reece!" Faith jumped out of the chair and flung herself at her wife.

Reece caught Faith and lifted her up, kissing her passionately.

"Take notes, Nancy, that's a kiss."

Alicia's eyes widened as she drank in the length of Reece's body. Her shirt hugged her perfectly sculpted torso and her jeans seemed made just for her. Her ass, and those legs.... Alicia couldn't blink. Suddenly, she was pinned to the spot by incredibly blue eyes, and her heart pounded hard.

Reece released Faith and took one long step in front of Alicia. "I'm Reece." She held out her hand.

Alicia was rooted to the spot, her legs feeling unbelievably heavy.

"Told you she'd dirty her panties."

Faith snickered and Reece looked toward her and winked.

Reece withdrew her hand and purposely stared at the stricken woman. "So, you're the lucky woman who fucks my wife." She narrowed her eyes dangerously.

Alicia nodded. "Yes."

"You know, Alicia," Reece stepped even closer, invading every inch of Alicia's personal space. "I don't really share well, but I suppose I'll let it slide this time, as long as you don't leave a mark. Every inch of that woman is mine and you wouldn't want me to get angry."

Alicia blinked rapidly and shook her head. "No, I wouldn't."

Faith bit back laughter and John kept elbowing her to be quiet.

Reece turned toward Faith and grinned for a split second, then turned back around. "You are playing nice with her, aren't you?"

The stricken actress nodded rapidly, unable to take her eyes off Reece.

"Oh, and Alicia, I don't think they're anything like cantaloupes." She looked suggestively at Faith's breasts. "They're too soft."

Alicia grimaced.

Faith bit her lip and John turned away.

Reece cocked her head and chuckled. "Pleasure meeting you."

Alicia ran out of the van.

Faith took Reece by the hand and laughed out loud. "How did you know?"

"I wanted to come see you and had to call Cori for the address. She told me everything. Why didn't you tell me Alicia was such a cunt?"

John grabbed his chest. "Ack! The C word!"

"A moment please?" Reece asked him and smiled as he left.

"I didn't have the chance and I didn't want you coming here all crazy to threaten her."

"Did I?"

Faith kissed Reece sweetly. "No, you weren't crazy. You were perfect. Now maybe I'll get some work done with her."

Reece stared at the door, something obviously on her mind. Faith took a guess at what it was. "No, she doesn't turn me on and I feel nothing when I'm with her."

Reece wrapped both arms around Faith and kissed her hard. They were still wrapped around one another when John came back.

"Break it up ladies and lesbians, it's almost time and now I need to fix her lipstick."

Reece sucked Faith's top lip and growled. "They should make flavored lipstick."

John rolled his eyes. "Then I'd never pry you two apart. Let's go, Spike, the lady has a scene."

Reece let go and stood. "How much longer are you going to be?"

Faith shrugged. "Depends on how many takes they need."

"All right then, I'll just have to keep John company until you're done."

John looked at Faith in desperation. "Please make it in one take."

†

Alicia waited for Faith, her mind swimming. She'd seen pictures of Faith's wife, read enough about her to feel as if she knew her, but seeing her in the flesh—wow. Her mouth went dry as she recalled those crystal blue eyes boring into her. Her mind swam with the image of the tall, muscular woman and she heard herself groan. She quickly looked around and snapped herself out of the daze. *What the hell is going on?*

†

Reece occupied herself by torturing John. He was such an easy target. She sat in the make-up chair and threw her feet on the small counter.

"So, John, how's it hangin'?"

John rolled his eyes. "It's not. I'm wearing underwear."

"I bet they're frilly," Reece teased.

"For your information, they're boxer briefs." The make-up artist stuck out his chin.

"Man panties. I'm impressed." Reece brought her legs down and stared at John.

John cleared his throat nervously. "What do you wear?"

Reece stood up and unzipped her pants, displaying the elastic to her underwear.

"Ooo, J.Crew. I don't like them, they don't have a hole and they're too tight. They squeeze my balls."

"Yeah, well, these are my dress up drawers. I usually wear Joe Boxer. They're cotton. I can work out better in those."

John unzipped his pants and showed off his Joe Boxers.

Faith entered the trailer and giggled. "All right, whose is bigger?"

John zipped up his pants. "Hers."

Reece chuckled. "Just comparing drawers. What's going on? Are you done already?"

"Nah, I forgot something. By the way, Reece, Alicia is slightly dazed."

Reece smirked. "I scared her, huh?"

Faith shook her head. "I don't think so. I think she's hot for you."

John yelled. "*What*? That homophobic twat?"

Faith grinned. "I think so."

Reece chuckled. "This can work in your favor, babe."

Faith pursed her lips. "Maybe. We'll see."

†

Alicia couldn't help it. Every time she looked at Faith, she saw Reece standing there in that skin tight shirt. Alicia wanted to reach out and touch those well-defined muscular arms. Her heart started to pound with fear as she imagined herself doing so. Why was she thinking these things?

"Alicia! Are you even listening to me?

The daydreaming actress shook her head. "Oh, yeah. What?"

Faith narrowed her eyes. "Look, make this easy, get in the car and let's go!"

Alicia frowned. Daydreaming about a woman? She didn't know whether to be disgusted or hot. Confused, she went and took her place, shaking off the disturbing thoughts.

Faith relaxed after the scene was shot and scrambled to get back to the trailer.

"Faith, wait up!"

"Alicia, I just want to get home."

"Oh, you have plans for tonight?"

Faith cocked her head. "Since when do you care what I'm doing?"

"Can't I be interested?" Alicia shrugged.

Faith smiled. "Yeah, I have plans. I'm going to fuck my wife."

Alicia's eyes widened.

Faith was confused. No sarcastic remark? No disparaging lesbo comment?

"So, uh, you and her, you know…fuck?"

Faith's eyes opened extremely wide. "Yes," she answered, curious to know where the actress was going with this.

"Like with a dick and everything?"

Faith replied hesitantly. "Yes."

Alicia looked to be concentrating. "I suppose she's the guy."

Faith was becoming annoyed. "Why are you asking me all these questions? Do you want to fuck my wife?"

Alicia physically jumped. "*No!* No way, I'm not a dyke! I'm just asking. Don't get carried away." She looked around nervously.

Faith narrowed her eyes. "I think you protest too much. I think you want to be underneath her naked body screaming."

Alicia swallowed hard. "You're crazy." Meanwhile, the images Faith's comments produced made Alicia's head swim.

"Good. Now, me and my crazy self are going home."

Chapter Eighteen

Reece actually laughed out loud, and then looked around the diner to see if anyone heard.

"Reece, it's not funny. She's totally hot for you and now my life is going to be miserable!"

Reece chuckled.

Cori high-fived Reece. "I think we owe this woman a toaster!"

Faith pouted.

Violet smiled at Faith. "It could be worse, honey, she could be horny for you."

Reece leaned toward her. "Babe, it's not much longer. I think you can stick it out."

Cori nodded. "Besides, just think, when she's kissing you, she's thinking about Reece. How sick is that?"

Faith sighed. "There is a certain irony to it."

Violet agreed. "Yeah, you know, Reece can't help being so hot. Just think about how smug you can be that she's yours."

"Yeah. Alicia tortured you all this time, now you can torture her." Cori sipped her beer.

Faith thought about that, then smiled. "I think you have something there. Just this morning, I was a stupid homo."

Violet laughed. "Now, that prissy little bitch is gonna worship you."

Reece leaned back in the booth and grinned. "I could show up and fuck with her head, if you want."

Faith held up her hand in protest. "No way. That would only make things worse. She was so distracted today, she was impossible."

Cori stood up. "Well, I, for one, find it hysterical. I bet those sex scenes are gonna be a whole lot different now."

Reece stood, too. "Please don't say that. I don't need to know."

Faith warned Cori with her eyes. "Come on, let's get out of here. I have business to take care of." She wiggled her eyebrows at Reece. "With this irresistible one."

†

Reece lounged back in the recliner watching television, the remote in one hand, a beer in the other. Her long legs stretched out on the footrest, her boxer shorts riding up one leg.

Faith descended the stairs and spotted her wife. She stopped and sat on a step, studying her. The way the muscles played in her arm as she lifted the beer to her lips, her long sexy neck as it arched back when she swallowed, the sinews in her legs as she shifted them. Faith swallowed hard and grinned. She's all mine. Mine. Her gaze traveled up and down the length of Reece's body slowly, stopping every so often to fixate on a favorite part. A grin came to her lips as she rose and continued down the stairs.

That's right, Alicia, it's all mine.

Reece cocked her head in amusement at the look on her lover's face. "Come here." She put the empty bottle on the floor and beckoned Faith with a crook of her finger.

Faith licked her lips, crawled up, and straddled Reece. "You are so perfect," she said quietly, settling her weight in her wife's lap.

Reece grinned. "Hmm," she replied, dropping the remote and grasping both of Faith's wrists in one hand. "I don't know," she said, pulling her lover's arms above her head until Faith's body stretched taut. "I think I'm looking at perfection myself."

Faith shivered as Reece's calloused fingers slipped under her shirt and dragged across her stomach. "Thank you," she replied with a groan.

Reece pulled Faith's wrists higher until the smaller woman's back arched, then her hand slid up and toyed with Faith's nipple ring.

"Don't thank me." She twisted the ring and watched Faith's mouth fall open and a moan escape. "I thank you for giving me this pleasure."

Roughened fingertips scratched across Faith's chest to capture the other nipple and Reece watched the expression change on her wife's face as she squeezed it. "Oh, yeah, no need to thank me."

Faith shivered and threw her head back as Reece leaned forward and placed open mouthed kisses on her stomach.

"Mmm, baby," Reece hummed.

Chapter Nineteen

John and Faith shared a laugh in the trailer, unaware of Alicia standing under the window.

When Faith left, she rolled her eyes at her new best friend. "Alicia, what a surprise," she said dryly.

"So, is Reece coming today?"

"I don't know." Faith shifted from foot to foot.

"She just comes? She doesn't tell you?"

"Yeah. She's like that." Faith was getting annoyed. "Don't you have to change? I'm already changed and it's the last scene of the day. I don't want to hang around today."

Alicia knew from eavesdropping that Faith was going to hang out with a friend named Cori. "Do you have plans later? Do you want to go shopping?"

Faith's eyes widened. "Are you asking me to spend time with you in public?"

Alicia shrugged. "Yeah, why not?"

"No, thank you. I have much better things to do."

Alicia watched Faith walk away and smiled to herself.

†

"She's right up my ass, Cor. God, it's annoying."

Cori laughed. "I could think of at least four hundred women who would pay to take your place."

Faith growled. "I'll pay them to take my place. No, really, she even asked me what Reece wears to bed."

"She's curious. I bet if you answer all her questions she'll run out of 'em."

Faith sat on the floor with Thelma and Louise. "Maybe Reece was right. Maybe I should just have Reece scare her."

"That may be the only way to get her off your back. All kidding aside, it sounds like she's becoming a little obsessed."

†

Reece sat at the juice bar and checked the time. Her next client was a bit late and if she didn't show in ten more minutes, Reece was leaving. She turned on the stool and watched the door for a while before turning back around and finishing her drink. Hopping off the stool, she started toward the locker room when she banged into someone.

"Hey!"

243

Reece started to apologize when she recognized the offender. "Alicia?"

Alicia smiled devilishly. "Hello, Reece."

Blue eyes widened. "What are you doing here?"

The actress's smile grew. "I'm your client."

Reece narrowed her eyes. "Excuse me?"

"Yeah, I'm a little late, but, I'm here now." She gestured to herself. "Shall we start?"

Reece shook her head. "No, I'm done for the day. There's a perfectly capable trainer standing there."

Alicia stood in front of the taller woman. "I'm a paying client and I want you."

Reece pursed her lips in thought.

"Oh, come on, Reece. What's another forty-five minutes? What kind of PR would it be if you walked out on a client?"

Reece sighed. What was the harm, really? "All right. Get moving, I don't have all day."

Alicia beamed as she happily followed Reece to the weight room.

Reece rolled her eyes. "What are we looking at, ass, legs, stomach?"

"I don't know, you tell me." The actress spun around slowly, giving Reece a long look at the whole package.

Reece raised an eyebrow. There was nothing at all wrong with this girl's body. She was definitely in great shape, had a fabulous figure, and a perfect ass. An ass, which Reece eyed suspiciously. "So, let's get this straight. I'm a trainer, I will train you, and that's it. Any questions?"

"Yeah, do you think I'm hot?"

Reece shook her head in disbelief. "Any other questions?"

Alicia looked around at the gym. "Why are you doing this?"

"Doing what?"

"Training women. I know more about you than you think. I know your type and the last thing you need is temptation. You don't want for money and you already have a hot business. This isn't a necessary distraction."

Reece's mouth hung open. She wanted to answer, but couldn't.

"See? You think this is a good way to be surrounded by women who want you. It's nothing more than ego." Alicia stared at Reece for a moment. "Unless you do get busy with your admirers and Faith has no clue." She advanced on Reece. "Do you get busy, Reece?"

Reece stepped backwards. "Don't fucking insinuate, Alicia."

Alicia kept advancing until Reece had her back against a machine. She ran a finger down the front of Reece's body. "You are so fucking hot. I can see why they all want you. You can have any woman you want here and no one would know."

Reece took a deep controlling breath and grasped Alicia's hand, very hard. "It would benefit you greatly, if you never touched me again." She squeezed the actress's hand and watched her wince in pain. "First off, you and me? It ain't happening, baby. You're disgusting, and I don't find you the least bit attractive. Secondly, this is the last time you and I will interact in any way." She released Alicia's hand, which the actress grabbed and held with her other hand.

"You almost broke my fucking hand," Alicia said through gritted teeth.

"Oh, Alicia, I could have done so much worse." Reece narrowed her eyes dangerously. "You're playing with fire and I will burn you."

"I hit a nerve, is all. You think you're getting away with fucking these bitches behind Faith's back. She's stupid if she thinks you're not."

Reece growled and pressed her body into Alicia, backing her into the wall. "You so much as put that bug in Faith's ear and I will personally rip your precious little lips off. Now get the fuck out of here before I hurt you."

†

"That bitch!" Faith exploded.

Reece couldn't help but chuckle at her wife's outburst.

"It's not funny, Reece! She's so manipulative and obnoxious and I'm sure she's going to start all kinds of shit, now."

"Faith, I didn't do anything. What can she say?"

The actress growled. "She can say anything she wants."

Reece thought about what Alicia said regarding fooling around with clients, and her eyes narrowed. Shaking off the anger, Reece embraced Faith and kissed her on the forehead. "Why don't you take a long hot bath, and forget about it for now."

Faith sighed in her lover's arms. "Come with me?"

Reece grinned. "How can I say no?"

†

Reece pulled Cori into her office and closed the door. Cori looked confused. "What's going on?"

Reece sat in her chair and leaned forward. "Alicia came to the gym today."

Cori's eyes widened. "No way!"

"Yes, way. She flirted with me and I turned her down. She got mad and said she'd tell Faith I was fooling around with my clients."

Cori blinked rapidly. "But you don't—"

"Fuck you, freak, you know I don't!"

The dancer nodded. "Just checking. So, you have nothing to worry about."

"What if she starts spreading rumors around the set? Faith will have to defend me all the time. What if Faith believes her?"

"Faith knows better."

"But, just, what if?"

Cori grinned a little. "You could go and scare her. Just a bit."

"I tried that, but she didn't seem the least bit threatened. Trust me, I wanted to break her fucking arm."

"Hmm. What do you want me to do?"

Reece sighed. "I don't know. I thought maybe you'd have an idea."

"You can quit your job at the gym."

"Yeah, and look guilty as all hell."

Cori grimaced. "Right. Didn't think of that. Fuck it. Faith can handle herself with Alicia, right?"

Reece raised an eyebrow. "Just do nothing? It doesn't seem right."

"Really, Reece. What *can* you do?"

†

Faith arrived on the set to stares and pitying looks. She narrowed her eyes. "Fucking Alicia," she muttered. As she passed a small group of extras, they looked at her with insincere smiles. Faith held up a hand. "She didn't sleep with my wife."

"Louise! Get in here!"

Faith rolled her eyes. She assumed John knew better than to listen to Alicia's rumors. "Not you, too?"

John jumped up and down. "She's telling everyone she spent yesterday afternoon with Reece!"

"Yeah, she stalked her to the gym."

"What the hell happened?"

Faith plopped into the chair. "Nothing. She hit on Reece and Reece turned her down."

"That's not what she says. She says Reece was all over her, and she had to fight her off."

Faith sneered. "Stupid bitch. And they believe her?"

"Who wouldn't? You know they always drag up Reece's past in the rag mags, and with Alicia's reputation…it just fits."

"Shit. This is just lovely."

The door opened and Alicia walked in. "Did I tell you how delicious your wife looks in Lycra?"

Faith turned away from her so she wouldn't spit. "I'm quite aware of what she looks like, thank you very much."

Alicia held a hand on her chest and looked dreamy. "So strong and so hot. She has quite a grip on her, too."

Faith spun around, and poked the actress in the ribs. "Listen, Alicia, I know nothing happened between the two of you, so take your asinine rumors somewhere else."

"She told you nothing happened and you believed her?" She laughed. "Honestly, Faith, what do you really think she does in that gym all day?"

Faith gritted her teeth. "Get out of my face," she warned.

Alicia chuckled. "Please, you are so naïve. A woman like Reece is like a kid in a candy store in that gym all day. Half naked, lithe, young women, throwing themselves at her feet, swooning on her body. Reece eats it up like she's starving. I was there, sweetheart."

Faith growled and made a fist. John stepped in front of her. "Why don't you just take your malicious lies somewhere else and save yourself a smack."

"Oh, John, you're just afraid of Reece, but you know the truth."

"Get the fuck out of here, Alicia," Faith hissed angrily.

Alicia laughed her way out of the trailer.

†

Work was horrible for Faith that morning, with Alicia making comments regarding Reece and her prowess. Faith had had enough and was stewing in the make-up trailer venting to John.

"She pointed out Reece's palm callouses, and the cut she made by picking her cuticle. Either she studied Reece a long time or she has a point."

John's stomach grew butterflies. "You don't think..."

Faith threw her hands up. "I don't know what to think! I don't want to think that, but how the hell would she know about my wife's palm callous?"

"Faith, I think she's just doing this to make you crazy. You know Alicia. She gets what she wants and I don't think anyone has ever turned her down."

"Oh, great, you're really making me feel better," Faith steamed.

"No, I mean that since Reece turned her down, she can't let anyone know. She's just behaving this way to save her own reputation. She doesn't care what she does to you."

Faith sat in thought.

"Come on, you can't really think Reece is doing all that Alicia accuses her of."

The actress frowned. "I trust Reece. Really, I do, but there's that tiny part of me that knows Reece's intrinsic make-up. Before me, well, she would never turn down an opportunity."

"Faith, listen to yourself. You're falling right into her trap. I think the best thing to do now is not let Alicia see you like this."

Faith sighed heavily. "You're right."

"I know I am. Now, go back out there, shoot the last scene and play along. She'll be the one that's crazy when you're done with her."

Faith's cell phone rang and she grinned evilly at whatever it was she heard. "Ooo, that's just too good. Thanks, Cor."

John raised a curious eyebrow.

"Cori just gave me the best idea." Faith chuckled. "I'll see you later."

†

Reece was extra careful not to touch anyone in any way other than was necessary while she trained at the gym. Alicia made her nervous and the feeling didn't sit well with her. She felt like she was being scrutinized, as if she was guilty of something she didn't even do. She was worried that Faith might think the worst. After all, Reece's reputation with women was legendary. She did her work distractedly while thinking up ways to prove herself to Faith. She felt it needed doing.

†

"Cut!"

Alicia tried to push Faith away, but Faith had her lip between her teeth and wasn't letting go. "Hey!"

Faith sucked Alicia's bottom lip hungrily and groaned. "Just knowing you want my woman makes me crazy," she whispered before winking and turning away.

Alicia looked at Faith's back in shock. "What?"

"I've been thinking, why don't we have a threesome?"

Alicia's eyes bugged out. "What are you talking about?"

Faith held back her laughter at Alicia's expression. "Well, I can't let Reece have all the fun, can I? At least I can keep track of her if we're all together."

"Uh…."

Faith had to look away so she wouldn't guffaw. "Who knew you had it in you? Here I was, thinking you despised us lesbos and you're just one big fat dyke!"

Alicia blinked rapidly. "I am not!"

"Oh, I beg to differ. Ooo, wait until the rag mags find out about you and Reece! It'll be delicious mayhem!"

Alicia tried to reply but said nothing and stormed away in a hysterical huff.

Faith broke out in laughter. "I owe you big time, Cori."

†

When Faith came home, she was juggling many emotions. While Alicia grated on her last raw nerve, she sure got revenge by torturing her the rest of the day, and that felt satisfying. Then there was Reece. Sure, she trusted Reece, but Alicia gave her a tiny doubt and Faith felt disappointment in herself for feeling that doubt. Jealousy came from that inkling of doubt. She closed her eyes and took a deep breath, grounding herself as she opened her front door.

Smudge practically climbed up her leg when she walked in. "Hey, sweetie, where's Reece?"

"Up here." Reece's voice was low and sounded odd.

Faith glanced up the stairs suspiciously before ascending. "Reece? Is everything all ri...?" Faith was speechless. The room was lit by several candles, On the bed was a bottle of champagne, baby oil, and Reece, grinning in that sexy way of hers, a silky robe barely covering her naked body. "Wha... what's all this?"

Reece sat up and grinned wider. "It's for you."

Without hesitation, Faith peeled off her shirt and practically tore off her bra. "All of it? You included?" She climbed onto the bed and closed in on her wife.

"Especially me." Reece leaned back, her robe sliding off her right breast. "To do whatever you want."

Faith's mouth watered. "So, you're telling me, I can do whatever I want, with ice cold champagne, slippery baby oil, and you?" Her sex clenched at the thought.

Reece nodded, her eyes playful and seductive at the same time, and licked her lips. She picked up a votive and swirled the melted wax inside the glass holder. "And don't forget the candle wax."

Faith thought she might faint from the head rush. Taking a few breaths, she quickly stripped off the rest of her clothes and straddled her sexy wife. "Why are you doing this?" she asked, leaning down and kissing Reece's earlobe.

"I'm yours. Only yours."

Faith's heart beat rapidly and a sense of relief washed across her. Reece knew how she was feeling and was offering herself as proof. "I love you, Reece, and I'm about to show you how much."

Reece gasped, as the cold champagne dribbled onto her stomach, her abdominal muscles bunching from the sensation. Faith's hot tongue followed and Reece groaned loudly. "Ooohhhhh."

Faith hummed in delight, her hands gripping Reece's hips as she straddled her legs. She had been taking advantage of her abnormally submissive wife for some time and was rewarded greatly with loud moans, frustrated writhing, and the strong aroma of Reece's arousal.

"Faith, baby, please—"

"That's right, baby, it's me, your Faith." The actress lifted her gaze to her pleading lover and grinned.

Reece glanced down at the twinkling green eyes and plopped her head back heavily. "You're going to kill me."

Faith reached and snatched a candle from the nightstand. "You won't die, I promise. I'm having way too much fun to stop now."

Reece's eyes fought against her. She wanted to watch the hot wax spill so she'd be ready for it, but her eyes wanted to close from the feeling of Faith's wetness trailing up her thigh. Reece's will won and her eyes widened as the wax began to drip. She gritted her teeth and hissed through them as the wax dripped on her skin. "Fuck!"

Faith poured cold champagne on top of the wax, and let it pool between her breasts.

"God, Faith, I swear. Only you... no one else could ever... ooohhh."

Faith nipped Reece's extremely rigid nipple and shivered from Reece's groan. "I can smell how much you want me. I don't think I can wait any more."

"Then don't!" Reece whined, wrapping her hand around the back of Faith's neck and pushing.

Faith groaned and dove downward, licking and sucking Reece's entire pussy like she was starving.

Reece threw her legs around Faith and groaned deep in her chest. "Yesss, fuck…"

Faith wrapped her arms around Reece's thighs as she began to come and held on tightly. She didn't plan on stopping anytime soon.

Reece jerked uncontrollably, her muscles clenching, wordless sounds escaping her.

Faith slowed her mouth and tongue, but never let go, humming her pleasure into Reece's swollen sex.

"Faith! Enough!" Reece gasped.

"Mmm, no."

Reece grabbed Faith's hair in both hands and pulled, to no avail. Not wanting to really hurt her wife, she let go and started to dig her nails into Faith's shoulders. Her lover merely growled.

"No."

Reece took deep breaths and balled her fists at her sides, giving up the fight. She could think of a million ways to die, and since this would be the very top of her list, she let her tense muscles relax a bit and squeezed her eyes shut against the over-stimulation.

Faith swirled her tongue slowly around Reece's hard clit, running her fingertips up and down her sides.

Reece shivered and grunted from the dual sensations. "Ohh, Faith."

Faith slid two fingers inside her wife and the strained muscles grasped them. Her nostrils flared, her chin and face were soaked, and her own sex was throbbing. Not wanting to move from her paradise, yet needing relief, she began shifting her body until she was straddling Reece's face.

Reece immediately grasped Faith's hips and pulled her down to her mouth, drinking in the abundant arousal hungrily. Faith writhed on her face, and Reece groaned, spearing her tongue in and out.

Faith felt her orgasm rapidly approaching and renewed her efforts to bring Reece along with her. She sucked Reece's clit into her mouth and swatted her tongue across it in synch with Reece's oral assault on her own pussy.

Faith's stomach tensed, her thighs trembled, and she came, flooding Reece with a delicious onslaught of arousal. As her wife trembled and twitched on her face, Reece's body clenched and her legs spasmed closed, tightly trapping Faith's head in place.

Reece pleaded this time. "Please, Faith, no more."

Spent, Faith climbed off of Reece's face and flopped onto the bed in a panting heap. "God, Reece, that was...unbelievable!"

Reece lay splayed on her back, groaning as an aftershock coursed through her. "Don't touch me, not even your toe." She glanced at the foot by her head and closed her eyes. "Not a toe."

Chapter Twenty

The Lounge was as busy as it could be and by the time Reece arrived with a shit-eating grin on her face, the line waiting to get in was getting restless. She drove by on her bike and eyeballed the prospective patrons, all men, all ages, all horny. She chuckled to herself and pulled the bike into the garage.

Pepe, the attendant smiled and fawned all over the tall club owner, wiping the gas tank with a rag he pulled from his back pocket before pushing the big machine to a reserved spot. Reece grinned. Despite the little glitches, life was pretty good.

Sarge and Reece shook hands heartily as Reece passed her by. "How ya doin', boss lady?"

Reece nodded slightly. "Pretty fucking good, Sarge." Blue eyes scanned the area and spotted the bright pink hair popping up out of the crowd. Reece worked her way toward Cori, stopping only when she saw the dancer entertaining what looked like a bunch of businessmen. Reece watched for a few moments, and chuckled to herself as Cori talked them into a few bottles of faux champagne.

She checked the stage area next and saw the dancers doing their thing, crowds of eager men and some women waving cash their way. With nothing out of sorts, Reece took her usual seat at the bar, and signaled the waitress.

"What can I get you, boss?"

"Soda."

Reece accepted the drink and slipped off into a daydream, reliving some of the finer moments from making love earlier with Faith. She grinned, recalling how she stood in the shower picking wax from the most unusual places. She'd used hot wax with women before, but never had it used on her. She recalled the sensation with slightly narrowed eyes. Especially the way Faith would pour the cold, bubbly champagne on top of the hot wax right after it fell on her skin. Goosebumps broke out on Reece's body as she shivered with the uneasy thrill of being so exposed and vulnerable. She remembered how long Faith had teased her, the sweet torture of oil, wax, champagne on her back, her front, everywhere. Her velvet tongue tasting and licking all the right spots. It seemed like forever before Faith finally gave Reece the relief she begged for.

"Uh, boss."

Sarge's voice broke her from her delicious memories. "Yeah."

"Cori says you better come quick."

Reece followed Sarge's finger to the stage where Cori was dancing, seemingly unbothered. "What's the problem?"

"Dunno, but she said to get you right away."

Reece blew out a breath and made her way through the crowd to the stage. Cori danced to her and whispered in her ear, "First seat at the bar, baseball cap."

Puzzled, Reece allowed Cori to gyrate in her face while she scoped out the bar. She stiffened. "No, way," she said more to herself than Cori.

Pulling away with a jerk, Reece started angrily toward the bar, but stopped short.

No, stop and think first. Don't go off without thinking.

Cori's set was almost through, and Reece migrated back toward the stage, keeping an eye on the bar.

Alicia, what are you thinking?

Cori finished her set, collected some cash, and jumped off the stage. "Follow me, Reece."

They wound up in the dressing room, where Cori took her cell phone from the locker. Running through her phone book, she screamed when she found what she was looking for. "Get ready for this," she warned.

Reece watched, curiously, as Cori spoke.

"Is this Veronica? Yes? I have a scoop for you. Alicia Alvarez, notoriously straight actress, is at The Lounge right now. Yes, it's a gentleman's club. Yes, she's alone… tipping the girls like crazy. Oh look, she's just jumped on the stage."

Reece's grin was from ear to ear as she listened to Cori give the address, then she called John.

"Hey, Mary Jane, do you still have that guy's number from Queer magazine? Good, cuz here's the deal."

Reece wanted to grab Cori and kiss her on the lips, but there was a far better scandal about to happen.

†

Faith looked a bit worse for the wear when she entered the club, but wide eyed just the same. "Where is she?"

Sarge pointed to the bar, where Cori was sitting next to a nervous looking Alicia.

Faith laughed. "There's a bunch of reporters sneaking around out there."

"I know. Cori called them."

Faith high fived the bouncer and hurried to Reece's office. "That stupid woman!" she announced.

Reece shook her head. "I wanted you here, so you can see that I don't want anything to do with her."

Faith smiled warmly. "I know, baby, it's okay. I'm not here because of trust, I'm here to watch what happens. I know you'll do me proud."

They kissed once quickly, but once they tasted one another's lips, the kiss that followed was deep and passionate. "Mmm," Faith hummed. "Are you ready?"

Reece grinned lopsidedly, the effects of Faith's kiss still lingering. "Ready, or not."

They left the office—Reece heading to the bar and Faith standing back, watching.

Reece paused, just behind Alicia, and then stood next to Cori.

Cori looked up and grinned. "Alicia, I want you to meet my boss, Reece."

Alicia's eyes twinkled. "We've met, haven't we, Reece? Only the last time you were wearing far less clothing."

Cori rolled her eyes.

"Cori, if you'll excuse us."

Cori fought back a grin in order to look put out. "Fine," she said and disappeared into the crowd.

"Alicia, what a surprise," Reece said sarcastically. "What brings you here? The tits or the pussy?"

The actress smiled deviously. "You."

"Is that a fact?" Reece replied with a smirk. "Here, in my club, in front of all these people?"

"Who would expect to see me here?" Alicia winked, leaning closer to Reece.

"True. But be careful. I recognized you in that hat and big coat."

Alicia looked down at herself and back up at Reece. "I'm sure there's somewhere, a back room, or something where we can go so I can take off this stuff. You know...get a little more comfortable."

"I'm perfectly comfortable," Reece replied, gesturing to her own clothes.

"Did anyone ever tell you that you look delicious in a tux?"

"My wife, as a matter of fact. You know her. Faith? Remember her?"

Alicia frowned. "Must we talk about her? I'd rather talk about us... and what we can be doing." She reached out and ran a finger down Reece's torso.

Reece watched the finger and grabbed it as it neared her crotch. "I wouldn't do that if I were you."

"Why not? I know you want me, I can see it I your eyes. I can see how you look at me like you want to fuck me."

"Do I?" Reece released Alicia's finger and stared her down. "You think I want to fuck you?"

Alicia stood up and leaned into Reece's body, "You do have the equipment, don't you?"

Reece chuckled. "Do you think us dykes walk around all the time wearing a cock?"

Alicia's face got hot. "Well...."

"You got a lot to learn, girlie, and I suggest you go read a book or two before playing with the big butches."

Just as Alicia started to stutter from embarrassment, Faith walked to them.

"Alicia? What are you doing here?"

Alicia grinned. "Spending quality time with Reece."

"Really? Did she take you to her office and show you what she's made of?"

Reece interrupted. "Actually, we were just talking cocks. Alicia here wants me to fuck her."

Faith pretended to swoon. "Ohhh, Alicia, the things she can do with a dildo, the way she works those hips, that ass..."

Playing with Reece was one thing, but having Faith approve was just weird. Alicia started to feel uncomfortable. She wanted Reece for some inexplicable reason, despite her being a woman, but not Faith. Reece was like a man in her mind. Faith was all woman.

"Well, Reece? Are you going to fuck her?"

Reece grinned evilly. "I wouldn't dirty my dick with her, baby. It's all about you."

Faith threw herself at Reece and kissed her. "Isn't she the sweetest, Alicia?"

Alicia, totally flustered, started to leave.

"Hey, where ya going? The night is young and we're just getting started!"

Reece watched her leave and Faith laughed loudly. "Come on, Reece, the fun's about to start."

†

As Alicia exited the club, a horde of photographers began snapping her picture. Cori, waiting outside, snatched the cap from Alicia's head.

"Look! It's Alicia Alvarez! In a titty bar!" Cori shouted. The people on line all turned to look, and the media was ecstatic.

Reece and Faith appeared. "Hey, Alicia, tell 'em what you were in here for!" Faith yelled.

"Fuck off!" Alicia yelled, trying to hail a cab.

"Man, she was all over those dancers. yep, Alicia Alvarez, with her face buried in cleavage. And man is she ever hot for my wife!"

"Yeah, and if you don't believe me, ask her about the birthmark she has on her right tit!" Cori shouted as a horrified, beet red Alicia jumped into a cab.

Reece and Faith turned to Cori with amused looks.

The media followed the cab a bit and the three friends headed back into the club.

Reece shoulder bumped the dancer. "How do you know about her tit, Cori?'

"We chatted," Cori answered with a smile.

"You're good," Faith commented.

"The best."

Chapter Twenty-one

John couldn't catch his breath he was laughing so hard.

Faith stood there, beaming and nodding. "Yep! She jumped into that cab like her ass was on fire. It was great!"

John snorted. "You couldn't have timed it better. The new rags come out tomorrow!"

Faith grinned smugly. "But the newspapers thought it was great for the gossip pages."

"What are you laughing at?"

Alicia's extremely displeased voice bellowed across the set and they covered their mouths to stifle the laughter. The trailer door slammed open and Alicia barged in.

"Look at this!" She threw newspapers at Faith.

Faith bit her lip to hide her glee. "Oh, look, page six, that's great exposure."

Alicia screamed.

John opened the other paper. "Just look how nice Reece's club looks in the picture. Gee, Alicia, you look a little startled, or is it guilty?"

"Fuck you, queen!"

John began reading out loud, "And rumor has it, young starlet Alicia Alvarez, was seen dancing on the bar with two completely naked women." He began laughing. "Oh, I'm so proud of you, you little lesbian minx."

"*Faith!* You did this! You masterminded this whole thing! I hate you!"

Faith held her chest in mock pain. "I'm hurt."

John fanned Faith. "Deep breaths, honey."

"You're both assholes. What am I going to do? How am I going to fix this?"

John rolled his eyes. "Please, you know you want to fuck Reece, so who are you fooling?"

Alicia swallowed hard and turned pink.

Faith shook her head. "Actually, the way she talks, she wants Reece to fuck her. Remember? Alicia loves dick." Faith laughed.

"Drop dead, both of you." Alicia stormed out of the trailer to loud snickering.

†

The last day of filming arrived and Reece made sure she was up to see Faith off. There would be some sort of low budget party later in the evening at an equally low budget club in the city. For Faith's convenience, Reece had offered her own club for the party, knowing Alicia would never show. It seemed, however, that more people than Alicia would rather not be seen in a gentlemen's club.

Reece was invited to the wrap party, but she was reluctant to go. Faith really didn't want to go either, but John talked her into it. After all, the major tabloids hit the stands that morning and it was sure to make the party extra juicy. Faith begged Reece to show up, and never got a definite answer. Reece still wasn't sure she would go. She hated these things, yet always relented to Faith, despite it all.

She despised premiers even more. Movie openings meant photographers and for the life of her, she couldn't get used to the incessant flashing in her eyes. There was one thing about premiers that Reece did like though, and it was usually the sexy dress Faith wore and how worked up she'd become just watching Faith walk the carpet.

Reece sat back on the couch and turned on the television, but didn't look at it. Instead, she lost herself in thoughts and memories. What she'd become and how far she had traveled to get there. She thought of Faith, with her infinite patience, understanding, and her love. Reece thought back to when she was a child, and how the word love meant absolutely nothing. She remembered her strong feeling of abandonment and how it fed her aggression and the terrible roads she wound up on and how Frankie saved her. Frankie began to teach her exactly what trust and respect really were. Cori taught her what friendship and caring was. Then there was Faith. Faith really saved her from herself. Reece smiled at that and sighed.

Smudge lifted his head from his curled up position on his bed and yawned. Reece chuckled. "Yeah, what a long, hard, day you had, little man. Come on, wake up, we're going for a walk."

†

Shortly after the director yelled cut, Faith was surprised to hear the rumble of a Harley approaching. She smiled instinctively as she watched Reece near. Faith began to trot toward her wife, as Alicia and quite a few curious others looked on. Reece came to a stop, swung a long denim clad leg over the seat, and pulled off her helmet.

Alicia's eyes widened when she recognized who it was. Her heart sped up at the vision of Reece running her hand through her messy hair as she took long strides toward Faith. She'd never admit it now, but Alicia definitely had a huge crush on the tall, beautiful woman. Her mouth went dry when Reece swept Faith up in a kiss. As if she knew she had an audience, Reece slid her sunglasses down her nose and pinned Alicia with a lurid leer. Wanting to flee, but rooted under the piercing stare, Alicia swallowed hard.

Reece licked her lips and cocked her head. "Hey, Alicia, you want a kiss, too?"

Snickers and giggles could be heard sweeping through the onlookers as Alicia stammered, "I...you— "

269

Faith winked at the stricken actress and patted Reece on the ass. "Gee, Alicia, after the other night I'd have bet money on at least a kiss."

Alicia finally found her tongue. "Fuck off."

Reece slipped out of Faith's embrace and sauntered toward Alicia, a devilish smile on her lips. "Come on, sweetie, give mama a kiss."

Alicia's heart stopped beating for a second as Reece grabbed her and dipped her. It began beating hideously fast as Reece kissed her right there in front of everyone. She swore she'd have a stroke. She flailed her arms, tried to scream in protest, but her body melted into Reece's arms and she thought she may have even groaned.

People hooted and hollered and some applauded. John shrieked in delight.

Coming to her senses, and with all the energy she could muster, Alicia pulled away, pie eyed and stunned.

Reece flashed a cocky grin, winked and strutted back to Faith, who was laughing out loud at the expression on Alicia's face.

Alicia blinked a few times, willed the butterflies in her belly to fly away, and wordlessly exited the set, to cheering and clapping.

Reece and Faith shared a laugh, but Faith refused Reece's kiss. "You'll have to wash your lips first, woman."

John snorted and popped open a beer. "Here, Spike, you earned it."

Reece accepted the beer, but spit the first swig out. "Driving, buddy, but I think this qualifies as washing."

Faith nodded.

Reece kissed her long and hard. "Ahh, that's more like it," Reece commented to the grins of the others.

"You're coming to the party?" Faith asked hopefully.

"Yeah, I oughtta be there with you, especially after that." Reece chuckled.

Faith smiled and hugged her wife. "Thank you, Reece."

"Come on, let's go home and fool around before the party."

Faith wiggled her eyebrows. "Sounds like a plan."

Chapter Twenty-two

"Reece, do you have your shirt on?"

Reece rolled her eyes and looked down at her bare chest. "Yes."

Faith poked her head out of the bathroom and narrowed her eyes at her naked wife. "If you're going to lie, at least do it where I can't see you."

Reece muted the television and sighed. "Faith, I'm hot, and it's going to take you at least another half hour to finish getting ready."

"Is that what you're doing with your hair?"

"No." Reece shook her head, ran a hand through her hair, and smiled. "Now, I'm done."

"At least let me spray it."

Reece growled. "Faith, just get ready and let me do my thing."

The actress went back to doing her hair, knowing all too well that Reece was going to do what she wanted. Miraculously, it would work out perfectly, as usual.

The blow dryer stopped and reluctantly, Reece rose, pulled on a sports bra, and her black jeans, then flopped back down on the bed to finish watching television. She craned her neck toward the bathroom and could just make out Faith's butt as she leaned toward the mirror to apply makeup. "What dress were you wearing again?"

"My blue one, with the thing, nothing fancy."

Reece thought about what dress had the thing and after imagining said dress, decided to wear her black button down, so she wouldn't clash with her wife. You can never go wrong with all black. When a commercial came on, she put on her shirt, took out her boots, and found the blue dress. She took the dress off the hanger, unzipped it, slipped her arms in it, and waited.

When Faith finally emerged, all made up, she grinned at her wife, holding the dress in the air.

Reece smiled back. "You look beautiful. Lift."

Faith lifted up her arms and Reece slid the dress over her head, mindful of her fresh make up. "Thank you, baby. Zip me, please."

"But of course."

Reece sneaked a kiss to Faith's shoulder as she zipped the dress. "You even smell beautiful."

"It's your favorite perfume." Faith air-kissed her lover and winked as she retrieved her shoes. "Come on, get your boots on and let's go."

Reece loved it when Faith dressed up, with her sexy dresses, and perfect make-up. To her, Faith looked just fine when she first woke up in the morning, but there was something extra alluring about her wife when she wasn't allowed to touch her. It was like a taboo and Reece was always bad with someone telling her she couldn't do something. Having Faith so close, dressed up, with stockings and hairspray, and knowing she can't mess it all up until later, made her want Faith even more. It was the only thing about public appearances that she liked. Driving the car, so close to Faith and not allowed to reach and touch her was even more of a pull for Reece. Sure, she could touch her, but with Reece's lack of self-control, one touch would not be sufficient.

"Are you mad I made you drive instead of Ted?"

Reece shook her head. "No. This way I can maul you on the way home without an audience."

Faith chuckled. "That was the plan. I don't know what it is about party dresses, but I like what they do to you."

Reece just grinned. "Parking duty is on." Reece never left her car with valets.

Faith diligently scanned for parking spots on her side, while Reece looked across the street.

†

Alicia nervously smoothed her dress and waited for her date to return with drinks. She hadn't stopped thinking about Reece's kiss all afternoon and her heart pounded fast in anticipation of seeing her again. She tried to ignore it, she didn't want to feel it, but at the same time loved the feeling itself. She'd had crushes before—always men—and she always got what she wanted. It was never as intense once she got them as it was from being next to Reece.

She loved playing with fire, and she knew enough about Reece to know she was an inferno. It thrilled her as much as it scared her. She could never pursue Reece publicly and Reece had proven that she would never cheat on Faith, but Alicia felt out of control when it came to Reece. She'd deny it adamantly, but the truth was she wanted that woman.

"Here you go."

Alicia accepted the drink gratefully and gulped it down. She studied her date, a young actor popular with the teen scene, and pursed her lips. She'd do him without thinking but she didn't want to for she was too preoccupied with Reece.

†

John was the first to see Reece and Faith come in and he ran to greet them. "You look faboo!" John kissed Faith on the cheek. "You look hot, too, Spike."

"Yeah, whatever." Reece shifted from foot to foot.

Faith backhanded her lightly. "She's so charming, isn't she?"

John laughed. "I'm used to her. So, did you see Alicia's boy toy?"

Faith scanned around, "No, who is it?"

John grabbed Faith's hand. "Come on, let's go say hi."

Reece sighed and looked for a corner to stand in while keeping one eye on her wife. She passed by the buffet table and stopped to put a few things on a plate for Faith to pick on, then went to the bar to get some drinks. She handed Faith the plate and a drink, pointed to where she would be standing and snuck through the crowd to her chosen corner. Reece watched Faith and John gossip, their heads close together, and grinned.

Faith was so much better at this stuff than she was. A product of her former life, Reece supposed, where they met at a country club for cocktails and tennis. Reece wasn't made for mingling. Faith and John began giggling and Reece smiled along with them. She liked it when Faith laughed.

She followed their line of sight and saw Alicia leaning against the bar lost in a daze, completely ignoring her date as he spoke. She watched with a grin as the two yentas approached the daydreaming actress and laughed out loud as Alicia startled so much that she spilled her drink on herself.

†

"Alicia, aren't you going to introduce us to your date?" John asked.

Faith handed the actress a few napkins. "Yes, where'd you dig him up from?"

The date looked offended but didn't say anything.

"Faith, John, this is Billy. Now you've met, go away."

John squinted at Billy. "Billy, are those sparkling azure eyes I see?"

Alicia coughed uncomfortably. "Really? I didn't notice."

Faith chuckled. "Have you seen Reece?"

Alicia's eyes cut right to Reece then back again. "No, I haven't even noticed her yet."

John snorted. "Hmm, that's odd since you've been staring off in her direction for a while now. Are you sure you haven't noticed her?"

Alicia glared at John. "No, I haven't." She pushed off the bar and dragged Billy away.

John and Faith laughed together before Faith winked and waved at Reece who nodded back.

"She looks so uncomfortable," John observed.

"Yeah, she hates these things. She only comes for the sex afterwards."

The make-up artist's eyes widened. "Sex afterwards? Always?"

"Always. I make sure she's not allowed to touch me when we go out to parties, and it makes her crazy. By the time we get in the car to leave, she's all over me. She comes with me to parties that she'd never come to, so we both benefit afterwards."

"Oh, you big fat sneak! I love it! How do you keep her from touching you?"

Faith grinned. "I tell her my lipstick will smudge, her callouses will rip my pantyhose, her ratty cuticles will snag my clothes, or she'll mess up my hair. It always works."

"I love you, Faith," John joked. "Let's go torture Alicia some more and shake that ass for your woman."

Reece ogled Faith's ass as she walked. She knew which panties Faith had on under her dress and imagined the actress wearing nothing but those panties. Her eyes narrowed as she fantasized and her mind began to wander. She stared off into space as she made a mental checklist of all the things she could do to Faith, with one hand, on the way home.

Alicia watched Reece discreetly, noting that she was daydreaming and knew by the lecherous grin on her face what she was daydreaming about. She shot a look toward Faith and back to Reece. A twinge of jealousy formed, and without thinking, she began inching her way into Reece's line of vision, slowly, so Billy didn't catch on.

Reece being caught up in her fantasy, didn't notice her at first, so Alicia took advantage. She edged closer, and closer, stealing long looks into Reece's eyes. A tingle of excitement inched up her spine as she stared into those crystal blue eyes, imagining them staring back into hers. Becoming bolder, she placed herself about four feet from Reece and made herself comfortable, all the while chattering with her date.

Smelling Alicia's perfume, Reece caught sight of her in her peripheral vision. Grinning to herself, she waited, fixating on a spot at the bar, watching as Alicia laughed loudly to get her attention. Enjoying the game, and waiting for the right moment, Reece played along. Finally, the actress turned her back.

Alicia jumped as a body was suddenly pressed up behind her. She attempted to spin around to see who it was when a strong hand on her shoulder stopped her. Her heart beat wildly as Reece's deep voice purred in her ear.

"I've been watching you."

Alicia swallowed hard while her date's eyes widened in question.

"I see what you're doing. You want me."

Unable to control herself, Alicia's eyes fluttered closed and her nipples tightened as Reece's breath blew across her sensitive ear. "Yes," she uttered.

"I bet you want me to whisk you off to the coat room, tear your stockings off with my teeth, and ravage your pussy with my tongue."

Alicia shivered visibly. Her date, not able to hear what this stranger was saying, looked completely confused.

Reece stepped back, allowing Alicia to turn around and face her. The actress's eyes were dazed and she licked her lips impulsively. Reece grinned deviously, narrowed her eyes, and let Alicia's imagination work for a bit. Blue eyes scanned the place for Faith, who was watching with one hand over her mouth and she winked at her. Faith winked back. Reece continued, leaning close to Alicia's other ear making sure the actress could hear her lick her own lips.

"Oh, yeah…" Reece groaned. "Can you just imagine the things I could do to you?"

Her body betraying her better judgment, Alicia inhaled sharply and uttered a small groan in response.

Reece, saying nothing, merely breathed in Alicia's ear.

Alicia's legs felt like rubber bands and she grabbed Billy's arm for support.

"Have you thought about it? Just me and you…alone…" Reece waited a few seconds, and then continued. "You know what, Alicia?"

The dazed actress shook her head as a response and her mouth went dry as Reece grabbed hold of her shoulders.

"That's never going to happen. I don't want you. All those things you just imagined I'm going to go home and do them with Faith."

Alicia tried to get free, but Reece wasn't done. "Now run along and play with your boyfriend because we all know how much you love dick." Reece released the actress.

Alicia's blood boiled. She had just been cruelly played. Her gaze shot around and she spotted Faith and John waving playfully and laughing at her from across the room. Furious, she screamed wordlessly, punched Reece in the stomach from embarrassment, and fled.

Reece laughed heartily, as Faith and John joined her. "God, that was fun!"

"She was just a boneless puddle of want and then her eyes flew open and you could just see the astonishment and the anger," John said through giggles.

Faith leaned heavily into her wife. "What the heck did you say to her?"

"Mmm," Reece wrapped her arms around Faith, "I described all the things I'm going to do to you later then told her I was going to do them to you."

"Oh, yeah?" Faith purred as Reece's hand slid up and down the small of her back. "Want to share one of those things?"

"Ripping your stockings off with my teeth."

Faith hummed in delight.

"Excuse me, lesbians, but I'm still standing here."

Reece and Faith stared lustfully into one another's' eyes.

"Ahem."

Nothing.

John smiled to himself, praying that he'd find his Reece one day, and disappeared.

†

Reece never did get to tear off Faith's pantyhose with her teeth since Faith shimmied out of them before they even left their parking spot. Reece's mouth watered, knowing what was waiting for her beneath Faith's panties. She slid her hand between Faith's already open legs.

"You're so horny for me." Reece pressed her palm firmly against Faith.

Faith moaned with pleasure. "Call me twisted, but I got hot watching you seduce Alicia."

Reece chuckled. "Dirty girl," she purred.

Faith leaned forward into Reece's hand. "Come on, baby, do something."

Reece let out a low growl. "I won't be able to drive if I start something now."

Faith covered Reece's hand with her own. "Then hurry home or pull over. I want you."

Reece could feel Faith's heat on her hand and her eyes narrowed. When the actress leaned her head back, Reece made a decision. She scanned the area and turned down a small street, pulling to the side and shutting off the car.

Faith grinned and thrust herself onto Reece's hand. With the smallness of the car, Faith knew there wasn't going to be any brave acrobatics, but she wanted Reece in any way she could have her.

Reece knew this and it fed her need to have her wife. She let go of Faith and reached around, releasing the actress's seat so she fell back flat. She leaned over the console as best she could and captured Faith's lips in a heated kiss. Faith's fingers laced through Reece's hair and she grabbed handfuls of it and held tightly. Their tongues wrapped around one another, sliding and battling back and forth. Faith propped her right leg on the glove box, it popped open as Reece cocked back her arm, smashing her elbow.

"Fuck!" she cursed, tearing her mouth from Faith.

Faith felt for Reece's arm in the dark and rubbed it briefly. "Ignore it... my panties... help."

Reece groped for the panties and yanked them down as far as she could, then out of frustration, tore them off.

Faith gasped, at the force and at Reece's hand roughly pawing at her heated sex. "Baby... God..."

Reece bit at Faith's neck, as her legs cramped and twisted and began to ache. She tried to adjust her position, hiking Faith up a bit on the seat.

The actress spread her legs as far as she could, urging her lover to take advantage of the invitation.

Reece blocked out her discomfort and slid her fingers rapidly through Faith's wetness. "You're so fucking wet and ready," she murmured into Faith's neck.

Faith groaned. "Fuck me, Reece."

Reece growled and plunged her fingers inside her wife, pausing for a moment to enjoy the feeling of Faith's muscles trapping her there. She worked her fingers in and out, quickly, knowing by Faith's slickness and the way her pussy grabbed at her that Faith needed it fast.

Reece took hold of Faith's bottom lip with her teeth and sucked it, making her lover squirm. "You really need me to fuck you, don't you?"

"Yes," Faith grunted, rocking her hips in time with Reece's thrusts.

Reece added a third finger and plunged them in hard. Faith yelled out and covered Reece's mouth with her own, in a frantic, open mouthed kiss.

Reece's nostrils flared as Faith's thrusting hips became erratic and her tongue froze. She leaned her forehead on the seat next to Faith's head and used her other hand to rub Faith's clit.

"Reece!"

Faith stiffened, then shook, her inner walls spasming around Reece's fingers. Reece's pussy clenched, and ached as Faith came on her hands. "That's it, Faith, you come for me," she whispered.

Faith collapsed into the seat and Reece watched her chest move as she caught her breath. She waited a few seconds before kissing Faith tenderly. "Faith, I can't feel my legs."

Faith laughed and tried to help the larger woman untwist her body back into the driver's seat.

"Ow… shit… my fucking leg."

Faith giggled as Reece threw herself into her seat and complained. "We could have waited until we got home."

"Bite me."

Faith grinned. "I love you, baby."

Reece couldn't help but grin back. "Next time, we take the bike."

Chapter Twenty-three

Reece and Cori waited on line at the supermarket and laughed at the tabloid headlines. Cori threw the magazine on the conveyer and Reece frowned.

"I'm not paying for that," she complained.

Cori rolled her eyes and dug into her purse, throwing a few bills at her friend. "Here, I'll pay for it. I need to add that to my "Alicia is a lesbian" collection."

Faith and Violet joined them, both women piling food into the cart Reece was trying to empty. Faith scanned the magazine and chuckled.

"After all this time, they're still following her around. I love it."

Many months had passed since they'd finished the movie, and every woman Alicia stood next to, spoke to, or even bumped into, was her new lover. Faith enjoyed it immensely, since she and Reece were no longer the focus of the lesbian headlines.

Reece emptied the cart and folded her arms across her chest, watching Faith, Cori and Violet leaf through the magazines. The girls tittered, laughed, made comments about each page, and leaned into one another comfortably.

Reece grinned at their fun and reached into her pocket for her wallet. "You hens want to start bagging? I don't want to be here all day."

Violet blew a kiss at Reece, knowing her bitching and complaining was just talk. Reece had to be cranky, it was her nature, and Violet knew the tall, frowning woman loved her.

Cori squeezed past Reece and started packing bags next to Violet, and soon they were hitting one another with the toilet paper.

Reece grumbled. "Jeez, how old are you both?"

Faith sidled up to her wife and hip checked her. "They know you love them, you know."

"Yeah, whatever. Sign the slip, I have to go help those dopes before they crush the chips."

Shopping trips were never Reece's favorite activity, and when it was with all the girls, it was practically torture. She snatched the bags from Cori and started repacking everything. "I don't want to carry three thousand bags. You can put more in this one."

Violet giggled. "You are such a grump! Lighten up. You're too hot to be that cranky."

Reece rolled her eyes and shook her head. There was a time when everyone she looked at cringed in fright but her worst look did nothing to these women. Thinking about it, it wasn't that bad that they weren't terrified of her all the time. It was sort of cool that they liked her as much as they did. Then again, there were times she couldn't get rid of them—like now.

"Ladies, and I use that term loosely, go open up the car and get out from between my ass."

Cori caught the keys. Faith started grabbing bags and leaned to kiss her wife.

Reece smiled. "You always know when to do that."

"I can sense the mood coming on."

Reece's smile turned into an all-out grin. "Let's get out of here."

†

Reece and Faith sat opposite Marsha and Quinn in the restaurant. Quinn fidgeted restlessly as talk turned to the opening night of Faith's movie. "Must we talk about this at dinner?"

Faith sighed. "Daddy, I'm just trying to invite you."

"Faith, dear," Marsha started nervously, "Um, your father and I decided that we're going to go out of town that weekend."

Reece raised an eyebrow. "You are?"

Quinn leaned forward. "We feel it would be too uncomfortable for us to be around. You understand, don't you?"

Faith nodded. "I do. Although it would be nice if you came, I understand."

"Don't think for one minute that we're not proud. We are. But you know...."

Reece rested her hand on Faith's knee and squeezed. "The content is too much. I get it. Faith gets it."

"It's not like a big time Hollywood premiere you know. It's a small theater and not at all a big event."

Marsha wasn't sure exactly what Faith was getting at. "Are you really okay with us not coming?"

"Yeah, I am. I guess. But leaving town entirely?"

Reece squeezed again. "Where you headed?"

"A cruise!" Marsha perked up. "We're going to the Bahamas."

Faith smiled. "Ahh, that's nice!"

"I can't wait. It's been a while since we went away, and you know how your father loves a cruise."

Faith smiled at her dad. "Just don't eat your way to the islands."

Quinn patted his belly. "I can take it."

Marsha laughed. "I'll bring you girls back some souvenirs."

"Thanks, Mom." Faith cringed inside, remembering all the ridiculous shell people and snow globes from past vacations.

†

Reece leaned her head back on the couch as Faith snuggled up, with her head in Reece's lap. She stroked Faith's hair with one hand; the other held the remote, flipping through the channels.

"Oh, stop there." Faith spotted a show she liked.

Reece stared at the screen for a while before complaining, "I saw this one already."

"I didn't, so deal."

Reece sighed and watched her hand glide through Faith's soft hair. It was blond and reddish and so silky that it slid right through her fingers. It was relaxing for Reece, even though she was in constant motion. She studied Faith's profile and the change of expressions on her face as she watched her show and grinned.

"You're right, baby, we saw this already."

Reece smiled and switched the channels again.

Faith took some time getting used to this flipping channel behavior, but now that she had, she hardly noticed it at all. She had gotten used to catching small glimpses of programs and Reece always stopped when she told her to, so she didn't mind too much. Cori complained that the constant channel changing made her seasick, but Faith took it as one of Reece's many quirky behaviors. She'd asked her mom if her dad did it, and she'd said he did, but only between all the sports channels. Reece wasn't discriminating. She was an equal opportunity surfer.

"Stop."

Reece pursed her lips so she didn't complain. *Bridezillas* was, in a word, nauseating. She studied Faith's features again, smiling when Faith giggled and her body jostled Reece's. Her hand began stroking Faith's shoulder, then her arm, then her side, making Faith squirm.

"That tickles."

Reece continued to tickle Faith until she turned in her lap. They looked into one another's eyes comfortably until Reece began focusing on Faith's mouth. She leaned down as far as she could until Faith leaned up to meet her. An innocent kiss became more and they wound up both lying on the couch facing one another.

Faith pulled away first. "Wanna fool around?"

"Do you have to ask?"

†

Reece watched as John dragged Faith off to the dance floor. It wasn't often that she went with Faith to a club other than her own and when she did, she didn't dance, so someone else had to come with them. Reece didn't mind, it gave her a chance to watch Faith dance and have a great time. Faith loved dancing, and she was damned good at it if Reece had anything to say about it. Her upper lip curled slightly as Faith danced, her sexy butt moving to the fast beat of the music. She turned her barstool so her back leaned against the bar and just watched. After some time, the two friends came back to join her at the bar, sweaty and winded.

"Oh, my God, Butch, you should get out there with your woman before every dyke in the place jumps her!"

Reece grinned, reached an arm out, and possessed Faith. "I'm not worried."

Faith laughed. "She just pissed on me."

"Nothing like a tomcat pissing on his property."

Faith kissed Reece quickly. "Only she smells better."

Suddenly Toni Braxton started complaining about never breathing again, and Faith pulled Reece out to the dance floor.

"Come on, baby, show 'em all who I belong to."

Reece grinned. Hating dancing was one thing, slow dancing was another, but wrapping herself around Faith always beat out the most unpleasant activities. She allowed herself to be led and embraced her wife tightly, touching her lips to the top of Faith's head.

Faith closed her eyes and rested her cheek on Reece's chest, feeling it move as she breathed down into her hair. She could be held like this forever. The safe haven of Reece's arms blocked out the world. The feel of her breath warmed her heart. The sound of her heart beating was better than any symphony. She was born to be in Reece's arms. She sighed deeply contented, and squeezed her arms tighter around her wife. The fact that Reece was up on the dance floor in the crowded club was a miracle. To feel her tall, tense lover relax in her arms was just heaven.

Reece kissed Faith's head, breathing in the scent that was only Faith. She, too, closed her eyes and swayed to the slow music, perfectly happy to be holding her lover. She relaxed and listened to the music, comprehending the words. She wasn't entirely sure if she could breathe without Faith in her life, and she was not going to find out. She inhaled Faith's scent deeply and kissed her again. Nope. She was never going to find out.

The End

About the Author

TJ Vertigo

Born and raised in Brooklyn, NY. Forty seven years old. Fronted an all-girl rock band. Did my time in Corporate America, but found my dream job working in animal care for the past thirteen years. I love my dogs like they came from my vagina. Love to travel. Cancer survivor. I'm a good thing in a small package. :)

Other Books from Affinity eBook Press

Bound by Ali Spooner
A rogue master vampire threatens the existence of the New Orleans vampire clan. Lord Jordan enlists Devin Benoit, sister of the Baton Rouge Alpha, and her witch lover, Tia, to assist with cleansing the city from potential disaster.

The Circle Dance by Jen Silver
Jamie Steele has moved to another town, trying to forget the heartbreak of losing her lover of six years. Sasha Fairfield finds her thoughts taken up with her ex-lover and thinks she wants Jamie back. Follow this captivating romance as love dances through the lives of these women to its surprising conclusion.

Search for the White Moon by Natalie London
Kathryn Austin, a government agent, is given opera singer, Adriana Desi, as her new assignment. Their lives and futures are in danger as the White Moon terrorists hunt them.

Immerse yourself in this fast-paced romantic thriller by debut author Natalie London.

Take Me As I Am by JM Dragon & Erin O'Reilly
When Jo Lackerly and Thea Danvers meet, an unexpected friendship develops, proving a catalyst for both women to change their lives irrevocably. Follow them on a journey of discovery that will have your heart smiling, blood boiling, and senses entangled in a wonderful romance.

Carved in Stone by Jen Silver
Join the characters from *Starting Over* and *Arc Over Time* in this final book from the Starling Hill trilogy. Ellie Winters thinks she might be going mad when the ancient queen wants a proper burial for herself and her consort. *Carved in Stone* has romance, adventure, a treasure hunt, and a happy endings for all, living and dead.

Anywhere, Everywhere by Renee MacKenzie
Gwen Martin's life in the Ten Thousand Islands area changes irrevocably when Piper Jackson comes into her life. Without trust, can the budding relationship between Gwen and Piper survive? Or will the answers to the questions continue to haunt them?

Venus Rising by Ali Spooner
Levi Johnson arrives at Venus Rising, an exclusive lesbian-only tropical resort in the Virgin Islands and finds more than she expected—a sizzling hot love triangle. Torn between her attraction to two women, she struggles to choose the right woman to share her life.

The Devil's Tree by Ali Spooner
Torn between her love for the pack and her need to find what's missing in her life, Devin Benoit travels to New Orleans. Will the previous happenings at the Devil's Tree help or hinder Devin in the fight of her life, and the life of Tia, the woman who now owns her heart?

The Beggars' Coppice by Erica Lawson
Edda Case is a woman in crisis who discovers that things are not as they seem. Is it truly a message for her from beyond the grave or is something more sinister taking place? Can Edda solve the mystery of *The Beggars' Coppice*?

Locked Inside by Annette Mori
How much does the power of love matter to someone who must overcome obstacles far greater than most people face in a lifetime.

Line of Sight by Ali Spooner
Sasha and her lover Kara are back. Continue the thrilling adventures of this couple from the Sasha Thibodaux series.

Requiem for Vukovar by Angela Koenig
Requiem for Vukovar continues the Refraction series and the exploits of Jeri O'Donnell and her partner, Kelly Corcoran. In an epic siege largely ignored by the wider world, Kelly, who was prepared to give up comforts and certainties when she became part of Jeri's nomadic life, encounters more than physical danger. Her ability to maintain her core integrity is assaulted by the inevitable ugliness of war. For Jeri, the true

battle is confronting her attraction to violence as she struggles against losing herself in the exhilaration of combat.

Against All Odds by JM Dragon

From award-winning and bestselling author JM Dragon, with significant updates by Erin O'Reilly, comes an original tale of romance where everything seems to be stacked against two women whose destinies bring them together. Life however takes a twisted path, setting both Steph and Louise in directions they never thought possible. Will love win out against all odds or will love be forever lost?

The Settlement by Ali Spooner

The outpouring of love and friendship toward Cadin helps her on her path to healing and learning to trust her heart to love once again. Join bestselling author Ali Spooner on this sensational journey that ends with a heartwarming romance.

Once Upon a Time by Alane Hotchkin

Raven only wanted to escape the blows that life had dealt her. She longed to be on the open sea and free. When she came upon a beautiful young girl sitting alone in the middle of a meadow, little did she know that her destiny would be changed forever. Will they become the pawns of the ancient vision or will both paths lead to the same port of destiny? Find out in this exciting high seas adventure that will capture your imagination.

Asset Management by Annette Mori

Follow the twists and turns to the explosive conclusion. Not everything is black and white. There are many shades of gray, and sometimes it's difficult to decipher who is good and who is evil. No one is all virtue or all malevolence, but sometimes love helps us rise above.

Do Dreams Come True? by JM Dragon
How do two people who really shouldn't get on end up in a relationship? Find out in this deliciously ordinary romance.

Return to Me by Erin O'Reilly
Will Salvation bring just that to Ellie, allowing her to find peace and happiness again, or will it have her questioning all that she believes in? A wonderful romance cloaked within an intriguing mystery.

Arc Over Time by Jen Silver
Book 2 of the Starling Hill Trilogy. This wonderful romantic continuation with the characters from *Starting Over* ties up loose ends. But the question is—does everyone have a happy ending? A must read.

The Presence by Charlene Neal
Can Rebecca and Kayleigh overcome ghosts from the past and their own insecurities, or will a presence from the past tear them apart?

A Walk Away by Lacey Schmidt
Sometimes chance brings you to the right person to help you resolve some of your baggage, and you learn to like yourself a little more. Kat and Rand are smart enough to recognize this chance in each other, but they also find that there is a

catch to every opportunity—walking toward something is always walking away from something else.

Possessing Morgan by Erica Lawson
The investigation has barely begun when Andrea becomes the target of a nearly fatal hit-and-run. But was it really aimed at her? Can she and Morgan find the common ground they need to solve the case and stop the attacks, or are the gaps just too wide to bridge?

Twenty-three Miles by Renee MacKenzie
This is a story about community, and how it comes together in dangerous and devastating times. When you don't know who to trust, you better have friends who will rally around you. Will Talia and Shay find the answers they need to the mystery of the murders on the parkway, or will justice be elusive? Will they survive their quest for the truth?

Reece's Star by TJ Vertigo
Under Faith's guiding, loving hand, will Reece successfully traverse the rocky road of emotion and embrace the positive changes in her life? Or will she panic and be unable to control that Animal part of herself? Will she take that next step to declare herself fully capable of love and devotion? This third installment in the popular series that began with *Private Dancer* continues the passionate and often hilarious romance of Reece and Faith as they both grow in love and in trust.

The Chronicles of Ratha: Book 2 A Lion Among the Lambs by Erica Lawson

Can Jordana believe in herself like her Noorthi sisters do? Only then can she fulfill her destiny as The Chosen One. Follow the colorful cast of characters in this action-packed adventure sequel as they traverse the galaxy. Of course, nothing ever goes smoothly when Jordana is involved.

Starting Over by Jen Silver
Book 1 of the Starling Hill Trilogy. There's a mystery afoot—whose royal resting place is disturbed at Starling Hill? All is revealed in this classic romance of simmering passions, anguished loss, and the wonder of love.

If I Were a Boy by Erin O'Reilly
Will Katie and Helen be able to make a life together work or succumb to doubts and the pressures of family? This story will fill you with the thrill of passion and the tenderness of love.

Terminal Event by Ali Spooner
Will the killer be caught or continue to evade authorities? Can Tally and Blair's budding romance survive the possibility? Read this intense murder mystery romance and find out.

Love Forever, Live Forever by Annette Mori
Fate intervenes and puts Nicky directly back into the path of her first love, Sara, and the corresponding events send her into a tailspin. Now she must decide—who will be the person she ends up living with and loving forever?

The One by JM Dragon
2015 GCLS Winner for Romance, Intrigue, and Adventure.
The One is a romance with everything, love, intrigue, misunderstandings with a happy conclusion—the only question—who gets the girl?

Confined Spaces by Renee MacKenzie
Corporate politics, complicated romance, and long distances conspire to keep Andie and Kara all boxed in. Can love triumph despite the Confined Spaces?

Reflected Passion by Erica Lawson
Through a mirror, Françoise embraces life anew, while for Dale it is a powerful awakening, forcing her to discover not only her sensual nature, but the inner strength she possesses.

Flight by Renee Mackenzie
Some lives will be lost and others changed forever when the sisters' lives intersect. Will they be consumed by the wreckage, or will they be able to pick themselves up and take flight?

Cowgirl Up by Ali Spooner
Ride along with the MC2, for boot scootin', butt kickin', dirt eatin', rodeo adventures, with a love story thrown into the mix.

E-Books, Print, Free e-books

Visit our website for more publications available online.

www.affinityebooks.com

Published by Affinity E-Book Press NZ LTD
Canterbury, New Zealand

Registered Company 2517228